THE FIGHTING FOUR

THE
FIGHTING FOUR

by

A. R. CHANNEL

THE CHILDREN'S PRESS
LONDON AND GLASGOW

PRINTED IN GREAT BRITAIN

CONTENTS

CHAPTER ONE

OCCUPIED NORWAY

OUT of the bitterly cold night they came, four white-clad figures, each carrying a submachine-gun, each helping himself along with a steel-tipped stick which he dug into the ice. Their feet made a little musical tinkling for their boots were shod with crampons . . . steel-spiked attachments which enabled them to move across ice without slipping.

When they began to feel snow beneath their boots the leader stopped and his three companions obediently moved up to him.

"Sergeant Harris, I've been thinking about the glacier. We hadn't bargained on it being so sticky to cross. It may make a difference to you and your three men."

"How, sir ?" Harris asked.

"It is a question of any wounded we might have," Lieutenant Barkly said quietly. "You go in first to clear the Germans out of the power station. You will have the job of holding the tunnel which runs from the power station to the village."

"Yes, sir," the tall, huskily-built Commando sergeant sounded a little puzzled.

"You are more likely to have casualties than the rest of us," Lieutenant Barkly explained, and went on more quietly: "I'm afraid there won't be any question of bringing wounded out. We couldn't get them across the glacier. See what I mean ? Once the Germans get wise to what is happening at their hydro-electric station they'll react strongly. What do you feel about it ?"

Sergeant Harris shrugged, then grinned as he said:

"Sound a bit odd if I said I'd rather go home, wouldn't it, sir. It isn't a question of ' how we feel '. We came out to do the job . . . we volunteered. I think you can depend on the men, sir."

"Good enough. I just wanted to know you grasped the position. I don't want any mistakes. Explain the thing to your three."

"Very good, sir."

A minute or so later, as they crunched their way across frozen snow, a little triangle of phosphorescence showed in the dark ahead. Lieutenant Barkly immediately turned back the collar of his anorak. Pinned there was a thin piece of metal on which was painted a similar luminous triangle. There were to be no code words. Either you showed the triangle or you risked getting a bullet.

As the four commandos hurried across the snow again there were a series of muffled clicks from the darkness ahead. They told of safety-catches being slid into the ' safe ' position again on a score of automatic weapons.

Sergeant Harris passed three holes in the snow, in which white-clad men crouched. In the fourth hole were his three. Slipping in beside them he laid his gun down on a piece of fur-lined waterproof material, then said:

"Curly, get the soup heated. China, unpack the crampons. We've an icefield to cross, a real stinker. Just like polished glass. When you strap those spikes on your boots, pull the buckles tight. You're going to have to dig in."

"Cig, sarge ?" Sam Foster had peeled off the adhesive tape around his one-time throat-lozenge tin which now held cigarettes and a supply of matches. You could always depend on Sam having dry matches, and smokes.

"I could do with a smoke but smokes are out. As soon as we've eaten we move. It took us longer than we expected to get across to the objective . . . and we can't waste time on pleasures."

"What is this 'objective', sarge?" China Brown asked, handing a pair of crampons to Sam. These crampons were steel spikes which fastened under the boots, they were sharp and strong, designed to enable a man to walk on the smooth, wind-blown ice of glaciers.

"Yes, it'd be nice to know what it was," Curly agreed, feeling at one of the tins of self-warming soup, now heating up nicely. "We train for a special assignment. We come across in a submarine that was about as comfortable as the last bus home on a Saturday night. We know it's Operation Lightning, but apart . . ."

"All right, cut it out," Sergeant Harris said. "There was a reason for not telling you. Suppose we'd been ambushed on the way up here. Suppose one of us had been wounded, and captured. Jerry has his own little ways of making people talk. See what I mean ? If we all knew . . . any one of us could have talked, and that could have meant death to the rest, and the failure of the show."

There was a moment or so of silence. Heads were nodded unseen in the darkness. Then Curly held something out:

"Here you are, Sarge: soup."

"Ta, I'm just . . . Ow!"

"What's the matter ?" Curly asked, all innocence.

"Matter . . . the thing's scalding hot. I'll bet the skin on my fingers is frizzled, you crazy loon. Why didn't you . . ."

"Nay," Curly protested. "For months you've

been training us to be Commandos. For months you've been drumming into us the idea that we shouldn't take a chance on anything. Why the first thing you said to us was ' All that glitters is not gold. Keep that as your motto and you won't go far wrong.' "

"Well, what the heck has that to do with you handing me a tin of soup that's too hot to handle ?" Ted demanded, licking his finger-tips.

"It didn't burn me," Curly pointed out, then added quietly: "I had my gloves on, and my woollen cap round the tin."

"Okay, smarty," Ted said, trying not to chuckle. "Remind me to think up some dirty fatigue for you when we get back. Now, where was I when that bald-headed Yorkshire tyke interrupted ?"

"You were going to tell us what the job was we'd come to do," Sam Foster suggested.

"Oh, yes. Well . . . Operation Lightning is the blowing up of a very big hydro-electric power station in the next valley. It supplies power to a big aluminium works. Shut off power and you shut down the aluminium works. That means less material for fighters and bombers."

"There aren't many of us for a job like that, are there ?" China Brown asked.

"You can't bring a battalion across to Norway

in a submarine, China," Ted said quietly. "Anyway, there shouldn't be much opposition. The place is very well camouflaged, and hard for bombers to get at because of the hills. Our Intelligence people think the place will only be lightly guarded. There is a snag. There is a village not far away, and it is connected by a tunnel to the works."

"Don't tell me, let me guess," Curly whispered, and wiped some of the hot soup from his upper lip. "We guard the tunnel!"

"After . . . we've pushed any Jerry guards out of the way," Ted agreed. "We go in first . . . overcome any opposition, and hold the place while the other blokes blow up the big water-pipes which supply the power, and the machinery . . . generators and water turbines."

"Any snags ?" China asked, draining the last of his tin of soup then turning the tin upside down and driving it into the frozen snow with one powerful pressing motion of his right hand.

"Could be," Ted admitted. "The glacier. If anybody stops one . . . the orders are we can't bring out the wounded. Couldn't carry an injured man over the glacier."

"So we go in first and come out last. Any chance of the Jerries getting to know we're there. . . . I mean if we manage to scupper the guards ?" Curly asked.

"I don't know. There's one thing you should be glad about . . . you've always moaned about having to queue back home, for pictures, and so on. Well . . . here you are first in the queue. You get out of the cold and snow first, and you stay there the longest. You're lucky to be coming with me, and don't forget it."

They finished a light meal. After the soup came raisins, chocolate, and sardines in oil; an odd-sounding meal, but chosen for giving strength and warmth.

A few minutes later the roll was called, equipment was checked: magazines for automatic weapons, hand grenades, and the all-important high explosives for the demolition work. As they stood listening to last-minute instructions they were like phantoms. To the north the Aurora Borealis flickered in and out uneasily, pale spokes of light wheeling across the horizon, and seeming to light up the whole range of snow-covered hills. Sometimes the wheels of light were white, sometimes pale green, blue and even rose pink.

The Commandos looked what they were, as tough a bunch of men as could be found in a day's march. Each was an expert in this type of warfare, and every man had spent grinding months of slogging across moorlands in the dark, swimming rivers in full kit, living off the land. They were quick on the trigger, and expert marksmen.

In silence they swung round into single file and began the march across a narrow, dangerous trail over the glacier which lay between them and the big hydro-electric plant. They were in the heart of enemy-occupied Norway, with a big job to do, and a submarine lying off the coast, hoping to pick them up in three days' time. If they failed to make the rendezvous they were to strike over the mountains for the Swedish border. Hitler had issued an order that commandos were to be treated as spies—and shot.

At ten minutes to midnight they were thankful to move off the glass-smooth ice into frozen snow, and a minute or so later were halted. They had another light meal, and were all glad of the chance of a rest. It had been hard and dangerous work on the narrow, natural track which went across the glacier face. A slip could have been fatal.

As they rested they tried to pierce the gloom of the valley. Below them, a thousand feet below, lay the big hydro-electric station. There was not a suggestion of light, and no sound save the low whining of the wind. The stars overhead were like bits of bright ice in the blue-black sky. It was cold, and no one was sorry when word was passed along to get ready to move.

Lieutenant Barkly had a word with Sergeant Harris.

"You know what to do, Sergeant? Any questions?"

"No, sir. No questions. I've got a plan of the building in my head."

"Good. Then it's all yours, and I wish you luck. If there is trouble and we have to separate . . . make for the coast and the submarine. If you miss the sub. . . . Sweden. Okay?"

"Okay, sir."

Sergeant Ted Harris stiffened, gave the officer a crisp salute, then turned on his heels to collect his three men.

"Got the rations, Curly?"

"You bet, Sarge."

"Spare magazines, Sam?"

"Yes, Sarge."

"Got the price of admission, China?"

A chuckle from China Brown as he fingered the hand grenades which were his speciality. He had one in each hand, six looped to his belt.

"Got one each for going in; one each for coming out. If they want any more than eight, they're greedy. I'm raring to go, Sarge."

"Right, now listen. At the bottom we take off our crampons. Fasten them on your packs, and then follow me. We go in quietly. We don't want to startle anybody."

"Not likely," Curly murmured. "Might waken
the baby, then there'd be trouble." He rubbed a
gloved hand gently over the smooth metal of his
tommy-gun, then began to follow Ted Harris
down the snow slope.

Even while they were taking off their crampons
in the level valley they could see nothing of the
power station. The roof was covered with snow
and the walls were painted white. The big
building merged completely in the landscape;
but there was one thing not even the wily
Germans could hide . . . the low purr of the
dynamos.

Aerial reconnaissance photographs had shown
that extension work was in progress. This was
going on at the northern end of the building,
and it was hoped that access would be possible
there.

Ted made his way towards the humming sound,
and located the building. He moved northwards along the white-painted wall until he found
what he was hoping for . . . a big doorway
through which building materials were carried
when the workmen were on the job. There was
no door, but a heavy tarpaulin sheet effectively
screened the place.

Cautiously Ted insinuated himself under the
stiff tarpaulin. There was a faint light coming

from a single electric bulb which he guessed was set above a doorway in the wall dividing the old part of the power station and the extension.

"Okay," Ted whispered, and wriggled right under the tarpaulin. Curly turned and flicked on his partially masked torch for a moment, pointing it in the direction of the snow-covered hillside. A moment later there was a single flicker of light. His signal had been seen. Now the men whose job it was to blow-up the big water-pipes could get busy, and the other demolition squad would come down with their charges of high explosive. They would wreck the turbines and the dynamos.

Inside the partially-completed extension, Ted waited. He was joined by Curly, China, and last of all Sam.

"Now, anybody want to sneeze, cough, sing a song or do a war dance?" Ted asked, slipping back the safety-catch on his tommy-gun. "Do it now, while everything's quiet. If there's a wrong sound from any of you after this . . . you'll be on jankers for a year when we get back. Ready?"

Three heads nodded in the faint light. Then four pairs of gloves were doffed, and though hanging by strings from their breast-pocket buttonholes, they were stuffed inside the belt.

They could be got easily enough, and would not swing if a man had to crouch low.

Three tommy-guns were cocked. China gently eased the safety-pins of two hand-grenades so that a slight jerk would whip them out.

"The bell goes for the first round," Curly murmured. "Come out of your corner fighting. Lead on, Sarge."

Sergeant Ted Harris was already moving. He was a big man, but he moved like a panther, his quiet, springy step taking him silently across the litter of material which lay about the unfinished new part of the power station. He reached the little door over which burned the solitary electric light.

The moment China was at his elbow Ted turned the handle of the door and pushed. The door swung open an inch or so, and brilliant light streamed through the narrow gap. Curly lifted his right hand towards his mouth and gripping the ring of the safety-pin of the bomb with his teeth he drew it out. Six seconds after releasing that grenade it would explode.

Ted opened the door wider and peered round it. The sound of the generators was much louder now, like the purrings of a crowd of mighty cats. There was a faint smell of oil. The floor appeared to be of asphalt, or it may have been linoleum. Everything looked clean and business-like, except the men.

Less than twenty yards from the door a dozen men were seated at a table. Before them were jugs from which steam drifted into the air, and there were packets of food by each jug. The night shift was beginning its supper. At the end of the table four German soldiers appeared to be playing cards, while another, a bayoneted rifle slung over one shoulder, watched the cards being quietly played.

The Norwegian workmen were eating and talking in low voices, the Germans were absorbed in their game. Then, and to the Germans it must have seemed like a bad nightmare, Ted Harris was there, with China at his elbow.

The German sentry started to look round as something touched him in the back, and if a man's eyes can pop out on stalks, his did as he stared at the businesslike China Brown.

There were gasps and a sudden end to the conversation and the card game as workmen and German guards looked up to see a British sergeant with a cocked tommy-gun at one end of the table, and a grinning China at the other quietly easing the sentry's rifle from his shoulder while letting him have a very close look at a hand grenade.

The sentry sat down at a nod from Ted, and was glad to take the weight off his trembling knees. A moment later Curly padded past the table on his way to the other end of the big room where a large sliding-door suggested the entrance to the tunnel which led down to the village. It was Curly's job to make sure no one interrupted the first few minutes of the invasion.

"Well, what are you waiting for?" China demanded, nodding towards the cards which were now held loosely in the nerveless hands of the four Germans. "Don't let Sergeant Ted stop your little game . . . he likes a hand of cards himself. Proper gambler he is. Go on, chum, is it your turn?" and he looked at the German N.C.O.

The N.C.O.'s face was pale, and beginning to shine a little as beads of perspiration gathered on his forehead and his upper lip. He managed a sickly grin as he said:

"*Ja* . . . *ja* . . . it iss my play. I . . . put thiss. . . ." He stopped as China shook his head impatiently.

"Not that, you clot. Who taught you to play . . . ? put the Queen of Spades on. That one," and he made the men about the table flinch as he tapped the Queen of Spades with the base plate of a hand grenade.

A yell from Curly, now at the big door at the end of the room, made Ted look round.

"All clear at this end, Sarge. Shall I leave the door open?"

"Only an inch," Ted ordered, "just so you can keep an eye on the tunnel."

Then Sam Foster, who had been guarding the small door through which they had entered, came up.

"Demolitition squad's here, Sarge!"

"Dee ... mo ... li ... shun!" Ted said slowly. "What school did you go to, Sam ? We . . ." He stopped and looked towards one of the Norwegians who had risen to his feet, and was motioning that he wanted Ted to go across to him.

"I speak . . . please . . . it is important."

"Sit down," China growled, and tossed the grenade in his left hand into air, catching it only when it appeared it must bounce on the table. The result was amazing. The Norwegians may not have seen a hand grenade before, but the five Germans knew what it was. They flung themselves backwards on to the floor, their chairs making a clatter. They knew what a hand grenade could do, and thought China had taken the safety-pin out.

When they scrambled to their feet at a yell from China, one of the men was bleeding profusely from a gash in the cheek. The rough heel-plate of one of his comrade's boots had cut him as if with a knife.

The Norwegian who had tried to speak to Ted

took the opportunity offered by the momentary confusion to jump to his feet and begin to run towards a small hut set against the power-house wall.

"Stop him," Ted yelled, after lifting his gun and deciding not to waste ammunition.

China slipped the grenade from his right hand to his left and *vice versa*. The one he now held in his right hand had its safety-pin in place. He swung his arm round as if he was bowling at cricket, and the grenade sang through the air. The Norwegian was within a few feet of the door of the hut when the grenade took him square between the shoulder blades. The man did not even yelp as he shot forward then collapsed face down.

"Bring him back," Ted snapped, and turned to look at the bleeding face of the German guard.

A minute or so later, while the demolition gang were moving about to various generators, China dragged the purple-faced Norwegian back to the table. He could not walk, and his hands hung down limply. China propped him on a chair, gave him a hard stare, and when he was sure the man was beginning to get breath back into his lungs said crisply:

"You got to get a long start on me, m'lad, before you have half a chance of getting away. And thank your lucky stars it was me, and not a

Jerry what stopped you. If we'd been Jerries I dessay you'd have got a bullet in the back."

The Norwegian, obviously in pain, opened his mouth, but no words came. After a minute he lifted one hand in a gesture towards Ted who was busy trying to staunch the flow of blood from the German's cheek.

"Get that paw down," China growled, "want me to give you a really good wallop? If I hits you again you won't bounce till you're a threepenny bus ride from home."

The Norwegian was not daunted. He still motioned towards Ted, and finally managed to gasp:

"The alarm . . . the alarm!" But Ted was busy and China was watching one of the demolition gang placing a charge of explosives carefully in a nearby turbine, having unscrewed an inspection plate.

Eyes, hands, even his quivering mouth registering the pain he was going through, the Norwegian nevertheless somehow managed to get to his feet. China turned, one clenched fist raised; but there was something in the workman's face which halted China.

"Here, what is it?" he demanded, and bent lower to catch the whispered words:

"The alarm . . . the alarm. In that shed."

"Says there's an alarm in that shed, Sarge."

China snapped, and at once Ted dropped his role of Red Cross man. He handed the first field-dressing to the German N.C.O., ordered him to carry on with the bandaging, then gave China a hand to get the Norwegian to his feet. They hurried him across to the hut.

The man gave a groan and pointed a shaking finger at a red light shining on a switchboard.

In halting English he explained that every half hour one of the guards had to come into the hut and re-set a switch which controlled the alarm system. If the switch was not re-set within two minutes of the half hour elapsing, then an alarm bell would ring in the headquarters down in the village.

"Why didn't you tell us?" China demanded, while Ted stood and stared at the red light, his face a mask of concentration.

"I try," the Norwegian protested. "You would not listen . . . so I run here to try to re-set switch before alarm is given. Now . . . I think it is too late."

"Re-set the thing," Ted ordered, and helped the pain-racked workman to reach up to the alarm switch. Then they got the man out and sat him by the table.

Ted knew there were only two ways for German troops in the village to get up to the power station. One was by the tunnel, and the other was by coming over a small hill.

Hurrying across to Lieutenant Barkly he told him he thought the alarm had probably been given, and asked that the lights in the generating room might be shut off.

"Sorry, Sergeant, can't do that. We need lights so that the demolition charges can be placed quickly in position. I'll get word to the men outside that they can expect trouble. You've got to hold the tunnel. Send the workmen out then they won't be hurt if there's any shooting. Lock the Germans up for the time being. You can let them out when you are coming out. Got that?"

"Yes, sir." Sergeant Ted Harris saluted and turned crisply away. From then on things moved swiftly. The Norwegian workmen were told to clear out as quickly as they could. The four guards and their N.C.O. were locked in a small toolhouse.

Ted went over to the big sliding-door which gave entrance to the tunnel. Sam Foster had been keeping watch there, with the door open the merest fraction. As Ted approached he flicked away the stub of a cigarette.

"Something wrong, Sarge?"

"I hope not, but there may be," Ted growled. "Open the door, I'm going in. Shut the door after me, but be ready to open it quick if I kick a heel against it. If I do that you'll know the Jerries are coming. I think the alarm's been given."

He stepped through into the tunnel, and the moment the big door was slid shut the drone of the mighty generators died down to a low purring. In that cold darkness he could hear the drip-drip-drip of water from the tunnel roof, the muted note of the dynamos and the turbines, and nothing else. Quietly he cocked his gun. If the alarm had been given there would be some scuttling about at this moment in the village as the German troops were turned out.

Several minutes ticked by, and then he became aware of a dying-down of the hum from the other side of the door. Putting his face against the woodwork he asked:

"What's going on in there? What's happening?"

A pause while Curly went to discover if something had gone wrong, and when he came back it was to announce gleefully:

"The dynamos are being shut down . . . so's they can put the explosives just where they'll do most damage. Leavin' one running to provide light . . . and so they won't get anxious down in the village. Got to keep them with lights in case they're nervous of the dark."

Ted grunted. He did not feel like laughing,

for he had a feeling that the peace of the moment would soon be gone. His premonition of impending trouble was correct. Within thirty seconds he thought he heard faint sounds from down the thick darkness of the tunnel. The sounds became clearer, the clatter of hurrying, iron-shod feet. Then the sound of a voice, amplified by the tunnel.

Ted slipped the door open a foot, pushed it back again, then nodded to Curly:

"Tell the lieutenant the Jerries are coming," he said crisply, and to China: "I'm going to push the door open in a few moments. Give 'em a couple of hard-boiled eggs to chew on."

"They'll love these," China murmured, his face a huge grin, and he whipped the safety-pins out of two hand grenades, then nodded: "Ready, sarge, when you are."

Ted nodded to Sam, and putting their combined weight to the door they slid it open a full yard. China stepped coolly into the opening and sent his two "eggs" winging their way down the darkness of the sloping tunnel.

CHAPTER TWO

"LEAVE THE WOUNDE

THE moment the second grenade l
China leapt nimbly to one side, even
Sam began pushing the sliding door
It was just as well he did, for the G
not slow to react to the light stream
that gap. There was a sudden "T
tat-tat" as an automatic weapon
tipped lead. The flashes of the explos
up the tunnel and revealing a squa
soldiers coming up the tunnel at a tr
  "Bup-bup-bup-bup." The bullets
the planking of the door, and whin
room. At a range of less than si
went through the woodwork easil
splinters of pine flicking into the air
  A second or so later the chatter
ceased abruptly, drowned by the
crash of twin explosions as China
the tunnel with a vivid yellow bla
flying fragmented metal.
  The door shook under the blas
Commandos instinctively cringed

the sound of the explosions seemed to be amplified in the confined space.

" Anybody hurt ?" Ted asked, looking anxiously round.

" Got my first wound," Curly said solemnly, and held out a splinter of wood. It was a couple of inches long and there was a trickle of blood starting to run down Curly's left cheek. "Went in like a needle. Think I'll get any hospital leave ?"

The other three grinned, and at a signal from Ted the door was pushed open a foot again. Ted was now down on his face, his gun poking round the corner of the doorway. He flicked a powerful torch on for a moment, and nodded. The two bombs had not gone far enough down the tunnel to do much damage. Two men were being helped down the tunnel, another was limping along. The rest were almost out of sight.

" Shall I give'm a little burst to speed them up ?" China asked, his hand fondling another grenade.

" You save those," Ted ordered. " We may need every one before we get out of this little lot. They'll be back, soon, don't fret. The Jerries aren't cowards."

Ten minutes passed, during which time the demolition squad seemed to be taking their time.

" I could have blown the whole place up by this," China fumed. " You'd think they was on a picnic or something. A dozen grenades would have . . ."

"They need more than grenades to wreck this stuff," Ted pointed out. "And when they do fire their charges . . . there won't be electricity from this place for a long time."

"But they're taking such a heck of a time," China protested. "Before we know where we are the Jerries will have flown tanks in from the Russian front to deal with us."

"You ought to be a newspaper reporter, China," Curly chuckled. "You got more imagination than the blokes that write books. What's the matter with you . . . getting the jitters ?"

"I don't like wasting time, that's all. If I . . ."

"Stand by," Ted ordered, and talking ceased. From far down the tunnel a light had flickered into being for a moment. Ted lay down, cuddled his submachine-gun for a moment, then loosed a short burst down the tunnel.

Immediately there was a flicker of winking points of light from far down in the darkness. The tat-a-tat-tat-tat-tat of a heavy machine-gun was like thunder in the confines of the tunnel, and at once there was an answering "Bup-bup-bup-bup-bup" from the partly closed door as heavy bullets began to smash into, and through the woodwork of the door.

The four Britishers stood aside, and watched while splinters of wood flew all about, and bullets ricocheted about the power house. The quietness of a minute or so earlier was gone now, for bullets were striking metal, and screaming off with that unearthly screeching sound which bullets make when they have been smashed out of shape.

The demolition gang halted for a second or so, then went on with their work, crouching a little lower, and making sure now that they had some part of the room's machinery between them and the big wooden door.

Within a minute or so there was a hole being eaten out of the centre of the door.

"Like as if giant rats were having a nibble, eh ?" Curly murmured. "They ain't half wasting some ammo."

"We'd better stop 'em, just the same," Ted decided. "I don't like ricochets. You never know where they go . . . and when they hit they don't half make a mess. Open the door a bit, Sam."

The door was opened a foot; but the Germans were not to be caught napping and the man behind the machine-gun was no fool. He guessed that something unpleasant was coming. He swivelled his weapon a little, and what sounded like a swarm of angry bees droned through the door as it opened a little.

"Give 'em an egg, China," Ted ordered. "It's too hot for me to poke my nose out."

China gave the Germans an "egg." He whipped the pin from a grenade, stood back and slightly to one side, then hurled it through the gap between door and wall. The small dark brown object struck the wall ~f the tunnel a dozen yards in the tunnel, and b~ ~iccu down into the darkness towards the wi ~ing, chattering machine gun.

A grenade can travel quite a distance in the six seconds which elapse between the fuse being operated and the explosion taking place. China had put all the power in his strong right arm behind that throw, and when the grenade exploded it stopped the German gun like a tap being shut off.

There followed thirty seconds of silence, during which time Ted had the big door swung wide open.

"No point in keeping it shut now," he explained. "They've shot a hole through it . . . and we may as well have a clear sight for shooting."

Hardly was the door opened to its full extent than two machine-guns at the German end began hammering away, the winking flashes of light revealing the tunnel sides and roof, and the men behind the guns.

Ted risked edging round the edge of the doorway to send a quick burst at the enemy. It stopped one gun for a minute, but the men down there were fighters.

There was a yell from the big room, and a minute later one of the demolition squad gave the news that Lieutenant Barkly had "copped one" in the arm.

Two more grenades were thrown down the tunnel, but the machine-guns did not falter. They were filling the air with the reverberating thunder of heavy armament, and when Ted chanced another look down his face went grim. The gunners were now working behind some kind of shield.

He gave the order to move away from the tunnel entrance, and to take cover on the floor behind some of the massive pieces of machinery, all slick and polished, and all silent now save one turbine and its accompanying generator.

The four soldiers edged their way backwards, and suddenly Sam was flung face down, and from that position he did not move. At the same moment there was a sudden commotion outside the building. Automatic weapons chattered away, and there was the crump . . . crump . . . crump of hand-grenades exploding.

"Looks like Jerry's arrived out there," Ted said soberly. "Hold my gun, China."

Hugging the floor he snaked forward and reaching out a hand grabbed Sam's pack strap, then heaved him slowly into cover. Something plucked at his sleeve, and as if an invisible knife had slashed at him a piece of the white material was whipped out of the sleeve and dropped a yard away.

"Miss is as . . . good as . . . a mile," Ted grunted as he hauled Sam to safety.

Then there was a shout from the small door which led to the unfinished part of the new building. In the past minute or so the demolition squad had finished their work and were on their way out to lend their fighting strength to those already in the open, trying to hold off a party of Germans who had come over the snow in an effort to outflank the saboteurs.

"We're beating it, Sergeant Harris. Come out as soon as you can. The first explosion's due in less than five minutes."

"Nice of 'em to tell us," Ted snapped. "Is Sam dead?"

"No—I ain't," and Sam, shaking his head as if dazed, made an attempt to sit up. "I think I stopped a shell with my back."

Ted took a chance and fired a long burst into the tunnel, and the Germans must have been in the act of moving their machine-guns nearer, for both guns were silenced for a couple of minutes. In that time, while the shooting, explosions, and shouting went on outside, vaguely heard through the closed and blacked-out windows, Ted sized-up the situation.

"This is going to be tough, lads," he said quietly. "Our blokes won't stay near this building . . . 'cause they know it's going to be blown to blazes in a minute or two. The Jerries will be waiting outside . . . there's more of 'em in the tunnel."

"Don't wait for me," Sam Foster said shakily. "I know what the officer said . . . the wounded has got to be left. Let my Mum know I'm not dead, will you ? I'll . . ."

"I'll smack you across the jaw with half a brick if you don't shut up," Curly Bates said tartly. "Nobody's said anything about leaving you. You start thinking how we're to join the others."

Sam nodded. He looked dazed, and after a moment muttered:

"What about the Jerries we locked up ? They'll have to be got out, too. Can't leave 'em to be blown to bits like . . ."

"Never mind the Jerry guards," Ted said curtly. "We've enough to do thinking about ourselves."

"Yes, but we can't leave 'em . . ." Sam protested, and was cut short by Ted. He chewed on his lip for a second, nodded, then agreed with:

"You're dead right, Sam. We can't leave 'em there. Wouldn't be decent. Curly, give me covering fire . . . as much as you can pour into that tunnel while I loose the Jerries."

"Here, am I listening to Ted Harris, or am I dreaming ?" Curly demanded. "Loose the Jerries, have you gone crackers ?"

"*Sergeant* Harris, if you don't mind," Harris said, a chuckle in his voice. "And don't forget that, *Private* Curly Bates; and we've *got* to let the guards out. They're going to clear the way for us, see. Come on, Sam, see if you can walk."

While Curly kept pumping short bursts of tommy-gun fire into the tunnel, making the air tremble with the stabbing tac-a-tac-a-tac-atacaca, Ted Harris and China helped the dazed Sam nearer the small door by means of which they had first entered the building. Curly held the enemy in the tunnel at bay, conserving his ammunition by making only short bursts of fire.

Leaving Sam and China by the small door Ted went to the toolshed where he had locked the Germans. He was aware that every moment now was filled with danger. It seemed a long time since he had been given the warning that the first explosion would take place within five minutes. Actually less than two minutes had passed, but the short hairs on his neck were prickling as he passed great solid-looking masses of machinery which before long would be blown to fragments of twisted metal.

He unlocked the door of the toolshed while asking:

"Any of you speak English ?"

"*Ja . . . ja . . .* I speak de Englischen," an agitated voice admitted. "Let us out, plees."

"In half a tick," Ted snapped. "Listen . . . in less than a minute this place will be blown sky high. You savvy that . . . ? blown up . . . high explosives."

"*Ja—ja-ja,*" the German agreed hastily. "I understand. Plees let us . . ."

"Get out . . . and warn your pals outside to get clear," Ted ordered. "Or there'll be hundreds dead, understand . . . hundreds. Now, beat it."

The Germans needed no urging. They raced for the little door and bustled through, hardly seeing Sam and China.

"Get through after them," Ted urged, and half turning, shouted: "Curly . . . come on, at the double."

Then he was helping Sam through the door. The five Germans were frantically pushing their way under the stiff tarpaulin which acted as door and blackout to the unfinished building where the extensions were to be housed.

The firing outside was desultory now, and there was answering fire from a distance, suggesting that the rest of the commandos had got away on to the snow-covered hillside.

There was a sudden burst of fire close to the tarpaulin, and a scream from one of the Germans.

Then a frantic screech from the German N.C.O. as he tried to establish his identity. If Ted had known any German at all he would have nodded his head and grinned at the warning yell of:

"Run . . . run . . . the British have mined the building. It will blow up in a moment now."

The firing outside abruptly ceased as every man who heard that warning promptly tried to get as far away from possible danger as he could. Ted Harris halted at the tarpaulin. On the other side of it a man was groaning. It was one of the German guards shot down by his own comrades who had mistaken him for one of the British raiders.

"No use going through there," Ted thought. "If they see us they'll shoot. They may have left someone." Aloud he said: "This way . . . we'll go to the far end of this unfinished place. We ought to be fairly safe."

At that moment Curly came racing through, and even in the poor light given by the solitary electric-light bulb it was possible to see the smoke still emerging from his tommy-gun barrel.

"Quick's the word, lads," he yelped. "They're on my heels. I just . . . hi, Sarge . . . you've missed the door. It's . . ."

"This way, and don't argue," Ted ordered, and hustled poor Sam along so quickly that at times he and China were almost carrying their "casualty."

Curly followed them, muttering to himself. He was a dozen yards from them, and twenty from the far brick-wall, when from the big room where the turbines and generators were housed came a sudden ear-splitting crash.

Curly hit the ground about the same time as his three friends. And all four had a momentary impression that the concrete was dancing. It seemed to lift into waves as if it might have been rubber.

For a full minute afterwards not one of them had any clear idea of what went on except that their ears were shocked by the thundering reverberations of titanic explosions which ripped apart the beautiful turbines and mighty generators. The demolition squad may have taken their time in laying their explosive charges, but when they laid them those charges were laid in the right places.

The roof of the building went up in a thousand fragments, and great masses of frozen snow dissolved into fine powder. The night became like day for long seconds as one explosion followed another. A five-hundred gallon tank filled with lubricating oil burst and added to the terror by igniting and making the wrecked power house a sea of flame.

The four Britishers did not even look up. China Brown was counting slowly to himself, the first two fingers of each hand crossed. His eyes were shut tight. Sam Foster lay flat with Ted Harris partly across him. Curly was face down, and chewing the nail of his left-hand forefinger.

Something monstrously big crashed through the brick wall which divided the new part from the power house. It sailed over the heads of the four prostrate figures, taking with it a wave of very hot air. Almost immediately there was a devastating crash from the end wall, and then a wave of cold air blew in.

"Up," Ted Harris had been lying like the other three, but he had also been thinking. He knew that a great deal of debris had been blown hundreds of feet into the air. In addition to parts of machinery there would be pieces of the roof . . . perhaps slates, or tiles, which when they came down could be as deadly as shrapnel. "Up, come on, and run." He jerked Sam to his feet and as if they had been his shadows, Curly Bates and China Brown also got to their feet.

They ran for a great gap in the wall. The cover of one of the generators had crashed through the wall as if the double thickness of bricks had been so much tissue paper.

Like hurdlers doing a two-hundred yards'

sprint, the four went over the pile of brickwork, even Sam taking it in his stride. They did not stop until Sam collapsed about ninety yards farther on. By that time things were coming down, singing and whistling strangely as they catapulted down to the snow.

"Just say your prayers . . . those who know any," Ted gasped, "and pray as we don't stop part of a roof girder, or some other bit of stuff."

"Is it safe here ?" Sam still appeared dazed.

"Hark at him," Curly jeered good-naturedly. "Is it safe ? One of these days our Sam will walk into a zoo and get hold of a lion's tail . . . and he'll say the same thing ' Is it safe ? ' What's the matter with you, Sam ? Wake up. He thinks he's on guard . . . and having a quiet snooze inside the sentry box."

"I'm wounded," and there was a new, strange note of dignity in Sam's voice. "You shouldn't say things like that about a chap when he might be dying."

"The only thing you'll ever dye will be your hair . . . or mine, if I had any," Curly said. "Get your pack off . . . let's have a look. Didn't you say you'd had a shell through your spine?"

"It felt like it," Sam grumbled, and somehow swung his pack to one side.

Something warm and wet splashed on to Curly's hand.

"Can't be so bad, Sam," he said loudly, and was sorry he had joked about Sam's wound. He felt at the waterproof white anorak . . . feeling for the hole, or the slit, where a bullet had gone through.

To his surprise the material was not even wet.

"Where's the blood coming from?" he murmured, and felt at the bottom of Sam's pack. That was wet, although some of the dark liquid was already freezing into inch-long icicles.

"Here, use my torch," Ted urged, and forgot Sam almost at once as a Very light shot up into the sky, and bursting high above the snow-covered hillside lit up for a few moments a crowd of struggling climbers, several of whom at once stopped and poured a withering fire into the valley.

There was an answering barrage of rifle and machine gun-fire from the Germans below, and the night was hideous for ten minutes with the crackle of rifle fire and the tac-a-taca-tac-a-taca of machine-guns, every sixth bullet of which was a tracer . . . taking a blob of fire curling up the hillside at what seemed a ridiculously slow speed.

"Looks as if most of 'em made it," Ted murmured, then turned at an exclamation from Curly Bates.

"What's the matter?"

"Poor old Sammy," Curly grunted. "I didn't agree with that order as we had to leave the wounded . . . but orders are orders, and that makes it too bad for him. A badly wounded bloke would never get across the ice, would he ?"

"Don't be a fool, Curly," Ted snapped. "What orders are you talking about ? I never heard any order about leaving the wounded."

"What ?" Curly and China echoed the word.

"I said," and there was cold deliberation in Ted's voice, "I said that *I* never heard an order about leaving the wounded. Get it. I never heard such an order . . . and neither did you, Curly, nor you, China. Get that . . . we're taking Sam with us."

"If you think I'm too badly hurt . . ." Sam began.

"I don't think anything," Ted told him gently. "Don't worry . . . you're coming back with us." Then he stared at Curly who had suddenly rolled on his back in the snow, and was stifling guffaws as best he could.

"Sorry, Sarge," he said, when he was jerked into a sitting position. "I never thought you'd have been took in like that . . . Sam isn't even wounded."

"I am," there was indignation in Sam's protest. "I could feel the hot blood soaking . . ."

"If your blood is hot soup then I agree with

you," Curly said calmly, "You're not wounded, Sam. You stopped a bullet . . . you stopped it with two tins of self-heating soup. The bullet smashed the tins open and they started to warm up, just as they do when you open the top. Smell that, Sarge." He wiped his hand across the bottom of Sam's pack, and held out his wet fingers. Ted sniffed, sniffed again, then laughed.

"Yeah, mulligatawny I'd say . . . or ox-tail. Sam, it's better to be born lucky than rich. You might have bought one . . . instead we've just lost two tins of soup. Come on . . . we're getting farther up the valley. Those Jerries are going to get organised pretty soon, now. Then they'll start hunting for us."

"Why for us ?" Curly asked, getting to his feet and giving Sam a hand up. "They don't even know we didn't scoot with the others."

"Why don't you use your loaf, Curly ?" Ted pleaded. "What about the guards we pushed out just before we beat it ? Think they'll forget there were four of us left behind ? They'll have to explain what they'd been doing . . . and we're their alibi. Come on."

They moved slowly northwards along the snow-covered valley, while behind them the night was uneasy with occasional bursts of automatic fire from the Germans following up the rest of the Commandos. They were hoping to do some damage, and perhaps draw fire from the British soldiers and so learn where they were, but there was no answer from the darkness of the glacier.

The brilliant glow from within the wrecked power station had almost died away now as the oil burned itself out. There were other lights near the wrecked building, torches were flashing, and it was obvious that a substantial number of German reinforcements had arrived.

After they had gone some four hundred yards Ted began to whistle. It was a tune popular during the first six months of the war, when Briton and German faced one another with the Siegfried Line on German soil inspiring some bright lad to compose the lines of the song: "We're going to hang out the washing on the Siegfried Line, have you any dirty washing, Mother dear."

Ted whistled softly, and if any one had been able to pierce the gloom he would have seen that the tune had an effect on the three men following him. Very quietly they inserted fresh magazines in their tommy-guns and cocked the weapons.

Suddenly the whistling ceased, and Ted said: "Now!"

Curly, Sam and China had obviously been awaiting such a signal, for at once they flung themselves apart, dropped into the snow, and were in position to start firing. The "Siegfried Line" tune was an agreed signal, and said quite plainly: "We are being followed, get ready to fight."

Invisible in the snow, their white anoraks and overalls blending perfectly, the four Commandos waited, fingers already taking the first pressure on triggers. Four pairs of eyes searched the silent landscape, and three men waited either a move from the darkness or a command from their leader, Sergeant Ted Harris.

The silence seemed to grow almost solid; it was like a blanket covering everything. To the four soldiers it seemed as if the stars grew brighter, so that each of them felt as if he must be clearly visible to the unseen enemy. Curly, China and Sam were sure there was an enemy near. Though they joked at times about Ted they knew he seldom made mistakes. He had decided there was danger . . . that meant Germans nearby, perhaps following them, and Ted's ears were sharp. He *had* heard something.

Then, when it began to appear as if the burly sergeant had perhaps made a mistake, a voice broke the brooding stillness:

"Stay still and do not shoot. Make a sound now and you die."

CHAPTER THREE

ESCAPE ROUTE CUT

THE night was cold, and the glittering stars cast a faint sheen on the snow. It made the few, stunted bushes growing in the valley take on queer shapes, as if they were spooks, or figures from another world. Nerves already taut, tightened still further at that command—"Make a sound now and you die," for it was hard to say where the voice came from.

A minute passed, then Sam Foster spoke. First he cleared his throat with a little cough, then followed it with a plaintive:

"Don't shoot me, mister. I don't want to die."

Ted Harris strained to pierce the gloom. He was watching one third of the landscape, China and Curly were covering the other two-thirds. A touch now on triggers would send a stream of lead spitting death all around.

Sam was acting as decoy duck. It was risky. He might draw a bullet, but if he did the other three would see the flash, and avenge him in seconds. It was part of their own private training that in a tight corner they should each play "decoy duck" in turn. It was Sam's turn to-night, and though it might mean death, or wounds, he did not falter.

There was no response from the darkness, and Sam was steeling himself to get to his feet, and call again, when the unseen challenger spoke once more, staggering the four Commandos with his:

"I come out . . . with my hands up. Do not shoot."

If he had said he was coming out riding on an elephant he could not have surprised the men more completely. They had been certain they were up against a German patrol. They had been ready to fight it out; and now the *enemy* was offering to surrender.

From a dozen yards away a shadow lifted itself from the snow, and a mist of fine white particles drifted down on the wind as the man shook himself. He had been covered with snow, and now that he rid himself of his camouflage he stood out as a dark blur, growing clearer as he came over.

"Who are you?" Ted asked, not moving an inch, and keeping the man covered all the time.

"I am Nels Larssen," was the reply. "I am Norwegian who tell you about alarm signal in power station. I offer apologies for saying what I did . . . but if you had started shooting

—then the Germans would have come and we all would have died—perhaps unpleasantly."

"Unpleasantly!" Curly chuckled a trifle grimly. "I never heard of anybody dying any other way in war-time."

"To die by shooting is quick, and clean," Larssen said quietly, "To die in the hands of the S.S. men is different. That is why I say . . . we might have died unpleasantly."

"All right, cut the small talk," Ted ordered. "What are you doing here ? You were told to get down to the village when we set you free. Why didn't you obey orders ?"

"And die ?" Larssen said bitterly. "Do you think the German corporal would forget I am man who tried to stop alarm bell ringing ? He knew what I did. He knew I told you about alarm bell. So . . . what do you think happen to me when morning comes, eh ?"

"That sounds reasonable enough," Curly murmured.

"I see you come up here," the Norwegian went on after a short pause. "So I follow you. I think maybe I return to England with you. May I ?"

"That makes one less for the Jerry and one more for us," China said.

"There's a sucker born every minute," Ted Harris snapped. "You'd swallow Blackpool Tower China, if somebody insisted it was a bar of rock."

"I don't get it," China protested. "It means one more on our side, doesn't it ?"

"If he's genuine, yes," Ted agreed. "If he was a fifth-column type . . . no! We can't afford to be betrayed, China."

"I do not betray you," Larssen said, a note of bitter anger in his voice. "I stay in this village as a workman only because I have old mother . . . if I had fled, then German S.S. men would have tortured her; maybe if they had been kind, they would only have refused to let her have rations."

"And why the change of heart ?" Ted asked curtly. "I suppose they could still torture her . . . or refuse to feed her ?"

"No, not now," was the quiet reply. "My mother died ten days past. So . . . I am free to fight. I have no relatives in village. I want to fight."

Ted was silent for a minute or so. The Norwegian's story sounded genuine enough, but Ted could not afford to take even the smallest chance. He knew how dangerous was the situation. They had three days in which to get down to the head of a fjord where a submarine was waiting to take them back to Scotland. They were separated from the main party, and there were Germans between them and the track over the glacier.

"You can show your loyalty to Norway,

Mister Larssen, by leading us over the ice . . .
by another route," Ted said crisply. "And don't
forget—I shall be just behind you all the time.
One wrong move . . . and you'll die before
you know what's happening. I'm quick on the
trigger."

"They call him Lightning Lou," Curly
whispered to China, who clapped a hand hastily
to his mouth to restrain a guffaw.

Larssen shook his head.

"Cannot cross glacier," he pointed out. "Only
one way over ice . . . and Germans on that
track now. I hear them shooting. They foll⁓
rest of your men."

"Could we go round ?" This from Sam Foster.
"I mean . . . round the back of the mounta. ⁓"

"There is no *back* to this mountain," Larsse.
replied. "Norway is mostly mountains . . .
the *back* of this mountain is over the Swedish
border, a long, very difficult way."

"We'd best decide on something," Curly Bates
said, picking at his teeth with a matchstick.
"Somebody's heading this way now . . . see
the lights ?" and pointed back the way they had
come.

"Must go north," Larssen sounded alarmed.
"German patrols search all district now. Perhaps
they know about you four."

"I'd say south," this from China. "They won't

expect us to head back towards the power station. We might be able to creep through that way . . . dodge down the tunnel, and through the village. . . ."

"Then you'd waken up in Heaven . . . or the other place," Curly scoffed. "You're not playin' with the kids on the corner of the street, China. Did nobody tell you this was a proper war. When Jerry shoots he doesn't *say*: Bang . . . bang . . . you're dead. He shoots and you *are* dead, savvy."

"We must go, please," Larssen pleaded.

"Wait a minute," Ted ordered. "You've given me an idea, China. We will go back."

"Crackers!" Curly muttered.

"What did you say ?" Ted asked.

"I said I could just eat some crackers, Sarge," Curly replied.

"Spread out . . . we'll ambush these Jerries, and no shooting until I give the word. Larssen . . . you stay with me. Do you speak German ?"

"Yes."

"Good . . . well, remember, if you say the wrong thing, you'll be the first to die. Now, lads . . . two over there, Sam stays with me and the Norwegian. Make sure you know where we are . . . we don't want to die from our own bullets."

Like shadows they melted into the snow, and the only movements from then on came from the advancing German patrol, the leading man had a torch which he flashed on to the snow, and it became obvious that the party were following the footprints of the Commandos.

Suddenly there was a new sound added to the crunch-crunch of feet on the frozen snow. It was the click of a safety catch, and a moment later Nels Larssen electrified the Germans with a terse:

"Stand still . . . or you die."

No patrol of soldiers ever obeyed a command more swiftly. The crunch of boots halted, almost as if the men had been expecting some such command. The torch light shone down on the snow. Then Larssen spoke again:

"You are covered by automatic weapons. Lay down your arms, and you will not be hurt."

There followed a few seconds of silence, and it seemed that whoever was in command of the patrol was weighing up the chance of their getting away if they showed fight. Then a guttural command was given, and there followed movements, the creak of accoutrements as the patrol bent to lay down its arms.

At Larssen's command, given to him by Ted in a whisper, the patrol moved forward away from the guns, and Sam Foster went out to collect the weapons. Then a torch was switched on, revealing six German soldiers, an N.C.O. and an officer.

Ted walked out, his tommy-gun at the ready.

"Anybody speak English ?" he asked.

"I speak a little," the officer admitted, his words clipped and jerky as if he were nervous.

"Good show," and now there was a chuckle in Ted's voice. "I always like to speak to the boss. Now, sir, you were looking for us, eh ?"

"That iss so," the German agreed. "We learn from our guards that four men are not with the main body. We find the footprints in the snow."

"Clever, these Jerries," China murmured, nudging Curly Bates. "They don't need police dogs, you see."

"When I look at them big feet of yours," Curly growled, "I wonder the Jerries dared come out after us. They must have looked like tank tracks."

China opened his mouth to say something rude, but left it unsaid for the German officer was being given instructions:

"Your men will hand over their helmets. We intend to march you back to the village. How far is it ?"

"March back to the village ?" the German asked, taken aback. "You mean you surrender ?"

"Don't jump to conclusions," Ted snapped. "The word *surrender* isn't in the British soldier's dictionary. Not at this stage of the war, anyway. And when we talk about surrender . . . it'll

be a German surrender. We are going to march
down to the village . . . wearing German uniform. If anything goes wrong you won't see
home again."

"But it iss impossible," the German spluttered.
"You could not hope . . ."

"We're not *hoping*, we're doing it," Ted interrupted. "Now, get your men to take off their
greatcoats. They'll put on our white anoraks and
trousers."

In ten minutes the transformation was com-
plete. Four British Commandos and the Norwegian Larssen were camouflaged in German top-
coats and helmets. The Germans, with the
exception of the officer, the N.C.O. and two
privates were in white. They were to march
between two files of *Germans*, made up of two
British on either flank in German uniforms,
carrying loaded tommy-guns, and a German
rifle, and the Germans were carrying rifles which
were not loaded. Ted walked at the head of the
little column with the German officer. He gave
that indignant soldier a last warning.

"Don't forget, chum, each of your men is
covered by one of mine . . . and these tommy-
guns just spray death at the touch of a trigger.
I'll have my gun muzzle touching your ribs at
the back. If we meet anybody . . . you say the
right things . . . or . . ."

The German officer gave the order to march, and the procession started south towards the wrecked power station. Somewhere above the glacier a German plane from a thirty miles distant airfield had arrived and was dropping flares in an effort to locate the retiring Commandos.

When Ted and his company were less than a hundred yards from the power station the night sky became alive with tracer bullets. The fighter pilot had spotted the Commandos and diving in at them, opened up with all he had. There were excited shouts from Germans at work near the power station and men who had been inside, trying to estimate the damage done, came running out to watch the show.

"Keep walking," Ted warned, when the German officer seemed inclined to slow down. "We're too busy for grandstand seats."

He cast a glance south east, where the tracer bullets were like tiny fireflies seeming to be curling quite lazily through the darkness. The far-off crackle of machine-guns was heard, and Ted and his three companions wondered how the rest of the bunch were faring. There would be no chance to dodge on that narrow track across the ice.

As they drew near the wrecked power station there was a sudden shout, followed by other excited cries, and Ted allowed himself a quick look up towards the glacier.

In the sky there was a red ball, which grew bigger even as he watched. There was a growing scream which seemed to make the night air tremble. The scream of a high-powered fighter engine at full throttle.

"He's been hit," China yelped, "he's coming——"

"Quiet," Ted snapped, and it was lucky that the blazing fighter was now roaring across the glacier, an awesome sight, with long flames streaming back from it, lighting up its wings. For a moment there was what looked like a ball of white far beneath it—the pilot had baled out—but the parachute was lost to sight after a second as the doomed plane screamed onwards, and then hit the glacier side, swung into the air for a few seconds, and then exploded with a terrific booming roar, the sound of which was echoed and re-echoed across the valley.

In the confusion which followed, for a German officer now began to bawl orders, getting men together to go out in search of the pilot, Ted and his men marched without hindrance into the ruins of the power station.

There were no lights now, and the beams from the torches held by Ted, Curly, China and Sam, revealed the terrific damage which had been done when the explosives got to work.

The mighty generators and turbines would

never work again. Most of them had had their covers torn off, or ripped wide open, and there was a litter of shattered metal all over the place. The roof had gone, and only twisted girders showed between them and the sky.

They reached the black gap where there had been a door covering the entrance to the tunnel. The explosion had ripped the stout woodwork to matchwood, and the wreckage lay yards away.

"Looks like we got out in time," Sam pondered. "Could have got hurt if we'd still been in here."

"*Could* have got hurt ?" Curly mocked. "Sam, you're the world's biggest optimist. You wouldn't have got hurt, Sam. Two things would have happened. Your clothes would have been blown off you, and a pair of angel's wings blown on in their place, that's all."

"Stop yapping," Ted ordered as they entered the darkness of the tunnel.

They marched down for more than three hundred yards, and walls and roof dripping gently, though here and there white patches of frost showed. Their feet, marching in time, made a sound like a battalion of men, and when they turned a bend in the tunnel a sentry was standing a yard or so away from the brazier over which he had been warming his hands a few moments before.

He gave the officer a smart salute, and looked

curiously at the men in white. He had not seen British Commandos at close quarters before, and wondered at their dejected appearance. Somehow he had been led to believe the Commandos were tough men, and not the sort to slouch along as these did.

When they were out of the tunnel he turned the handle of his telephone and warned the orderly room at the village headquarters that some of the British raiders had been caught, and were being brought in.

"They don't look very brave to me," he finished. "If these are the best of the Englanders I don't think there's any doubt about us winning the war."

The village street was grey even in the darkness, for there was piled snow on each side of the road. The roof-tops were white, and the star-sheen reflected from them, giving a vague suggestion of light to the scene. No lights showed nor did there appear to be anyone alive in the place.

"Straight to German headquarters," Ted ordered, and turning to Nels Larssen on the right flank, went on: "How do they get to this place ? Is there a railway ?"

"Narrow gauge, with Diesel engines," the Norwegian explained.

"What's the idea, Sarge ?" China asked,

"wouldn't it be better if we made a bee-line for the railway . . . instead of Jerry headquarters ? After all, what do we . . . ?"

"Want my stripes ?" Ted asked, a grin on his face.

"No blooming fear," was the quick retort. "I'll have 'em when we gets back . . . but not when we're up to the neck in trouble."

"Then keep quiet, and look out. That looks like the H.Q."

They had turned into a small square, and parked alongside a building slightly bigger than the rest were several lorries.

The sentry walking up and down turned at the sound of crunching snow and challenged them. The German officer answered without hesitation. Ted's gun muzzle in his back was a first class "persuader."

The sentry flashed his torch when he had ordered them to advance and be recognised, and was sworn at by the German officer, who was afraid the sentry might smell a rat and start something.

A stiff salute from the sentry and they were filing into the building. A dim light burned in the long, narrow hall, and a door on the left had some words painted on it. The officer had his hand on the door knob when there was a bellowed inquiry from upstairs.

Ted heard Nels Larssen gasp, and he lifted his gun to cover not only the officer but the nearest German soldiers. At the same time he asked:

"What's that?"

"Someone shouted: 'If those are the prisoners . . . bring them up for questioning.'"

"How does he know?" Ted asked, and the German officer shrugged.

"Perhaps the sentry at the tunnel rang through. Otherwise I do not know."

There was another impatient yell from above, and Ted nudged the German.

"Tell him you are bringing the N.C.O. . . . first." Then to Curly Bates: "Get in there. Hold everybody against the wall. See that no telephone calls are made."

"Okay, Sarge."

Ted turned to the officer, jerked a thumb towards a flight of stairs and then followed the man when he obeyed.

Curly flung open the door of what proved to be the German Orderly Room and went in with his tommy-gun at waist height. There were three Germans in the room, one at a telephone switchboard; one sat at a desk, and one in the act of pouring boiling water into a jug. Luckily for the latter German he was so busy with his task that the last drop of water had been poured before he realised that his two companions were on their feet, hands reaching for the ceiling, while three grim-faced men in German uniform menaced a gang which included four men who were clad in white.

"You'd better get to the switchboard, Larssen," Curly ordered, "and I dessay you'd better have the Jerry operator with you. If you answer any calls somebody might suspect. You—dishface—get back to your job."

The switchboard operator went swiftly to his seat and picked up a headset. At a command from Curly, Nels ordered the German to find a duplicate headset, so that he could listen to all incoming calls.

"What are you brewing, chum?" It was China who was sniffing the smell coming from the jug. "Smells as if it ought to be coffee, but there's something rum about it."

"Maybe they've got rum in it," Sam Foster suggested, his eyes lighting up. "Rum and coffee would be nice."

"So would steak and chips," Curly said, "but you've not a hope of getting that, either. That'll be ersatz coffee . . . which means acorns ground up."

"It'll be hot and wet," Sam pointed out. "Shall we have a mug?"

"Pour five . . . no : . . better only pour four.

Ted likes his piping hot, and he'll probably not be down for a minute or two."

"He'll smack you down if he knows you are calling him Ted," Sam chuckled. "Never could understand why he's so blooming sticky about being called ' Sarge ' all the time . . . he's such a good bloke."

"I'll tell you why, Sammy," China butted in. "He don't mind being called Ted . . . but if he let us keep doing it, one of these days we'd do it when one of the officers was there. Then the balloon'd go up. A sergeant's a sergeant, and you've got to keep discipline. Ta!" and he took the mug of ersatz coffee.

They ate some of the sausage smoking quietly over a grill, while the Germans watched in silence. There came the sound of feet on the stairs, and then the door was kicked open and a fuming officer walked in, his hands above his head. At sight of him the rest of the German soldiers clicked their heels and stiffened to attention.

"Change back in to your white clothes," Ted ordered, taking the mug of coffee. "Then see that every man jack of this crowd takes off his belt, boots and braces."

The German officer who had been in charge of the patrol, Kapitan Schloss, gave an apologetic cough, clicked his heels and addressed Ted:

"Sergeant . . . my Commanding Officer protests against this indignity. He refuses to do this while common soldiers are present."

"I shan't tell him again," Ted said quietly, and draining the last of his coffee he picked up his tommy-gun. Kapitan Schloss was speaking to the older man whose face was growing redder and redder, while he snarled and bellowed at Schloss.

"I am sorry, sergeant, but he refuses," Schloss said anxiously.

Ted whipped up his gun and swivelled on his heels, the weapon pointing at the Commanding Officer's belt buckle. For perhaps three seconds the two men stared each other in the eye, and it was the German who capitulated. He ripped off his belt, then began tugging at his jackboots.

"Collect the boots and things," Ted ordered, "and dump them some distance away. See if you can find some spot where they won't be easy to find."

"Sarge," Sam said hesitantly. "There's a sentry outside. Hadn't we better deal with him?"

"Good lad, Sam. One of these days, if I live long enough, I'm going to recommend you for a stripe. Yes . . . we'll have the sentry in here. He'll be warmer," and he grinned.

Kapitan Schloss shrugged dejectedly when told to call the sentry in. He spoke to the Orderly Room corporal, and that man went into the passage, Sam's gun at his back, and the sentry was called in.

The man came in perkily enough, but his eyes bulged when he found himself staring at the muzzle of a tommy-gun. He handed over his rifle and joined the rest of them against the wall.

Sam and China carried out the array of boots, belts and braces, and when they came back they were both a little flurried.

"There's Jerries in the square, Sarge," China said.

"On foot?"

"Just got out of a lorry."

The next minute was hectic. China and Sam were ordered to take the prisoners upstairs and lock them in the top floor. Only the fuming Commanding Officer was kept back. His face had lost its purple look now, and he was beginning to grow pale.

"You're our passport," Ted told him, and Larssen interpreted. There was no angry outburst now. The German was afraid. He realised it would be touch and go in the next few minutes. If someone came into the Orderly Room to report, there would be fighting, firing, and he would most likely die early on. He turned to Larssen and said something quickly.

"The German asks permission to stand in the

doorway . . . in case the N.C.O. in charge of the lorry tries to come in here."

"He's learning sense," Ted chuckled. "Tell him to send the men back to their billets, and if we get away . . . he gets away without injury."

The German went to the door of the Orderly Room, his legs wide apart to keep his beltless trousers from slipping down. A few moments later there was a kicking on the wooden side of the house as a German sergeant knocked the snow off his boots prior to entering the headquarters.

There was a tense silence in the Orderly Room. Ted stood just behind the German officer, his left forefinger sticking in that man's back . . . the muzzle of his tommy-gun just poking unobtrusively between the German's ribs and the side of the doorway.

The N.C.O. rattled up the front steps, and was halted at once by a curt command from the C.O. That he had not expected to see his Commanding Officer was obvious, and his tone was apologetic when he began to speak. When he had finished the Commanding Officer snapped out a short command and the man went out again. There followed one or two bellowed commands in the square, then the sound of voices as the troops who had arrived back by lorry started to walk off to their billets.

"What now, Sarge ?" Curly asked.

"As soon as they're out of the square we're leaving. Larssen, how far is the railway siding ?"

"Five kilometres."

"Five kilometres," Ted mused. "Er . . . let me see . . . how much is that in miles?"

"About three." It was Sam Foster. Sam was supposed to be a bit slow acting and thinking, but he had the answer pat, and Ted nodded approval. "Curly, you'll drive. Nels, you sit in front with the Jerry . . . and make sure if we come to any road-blocks that he says the right thing. I'll be in the back. China, got any grenades left ?"

"Three, Sarge. Want one ?"

"Give Larssen one. Larssen . . . you take this grenade. You put it in the Jerry's left pocket, keep your finger hooked through the split ring of the safety-pin. Let him see what you are doing. If you have to leave the lorry in an emergency you'll take the-safety pin with you . . . and leave the grenade in the Hun's pocket. Got the idea ?"

Larssen thought for a moment, then grinned. He took the grenade from China, held the trip lever while he withdrew the safety-pin, then pushed it back, conscious that the German Commanding Officer was watching him with horror in his eyes.

"Now, tell him what you are going to do,"

Ted ordered, and if the German had been pale-faced before he became even more so now.

"That makes sure we get through road-blocks, anyway," Ted chuckled. "Curly, rip out those telephone wire connections. I don't suppose that bunch upstairs will take long to get loose, and we don't want 'em ringing through to places to warn folks we're on our way home."

"I took the liberty of telling Captain Schloss that we'd probably be staying here some time," Sam Foster said, a twinkle in his eyes. "And I said that if we heard any row from upstairs I'd be up and relieve them of their pants. I hope I did right."

"That's what I call exceeding your duty," Ted snapped, and then with a grin. "Nice work, Sam . . . very nice work. I thought they were being quiet. Now . . . outside, everybody. Larssen . . . I think the General might be asked for an ignition key. I dare say he'll know where they are."

The German pointed to a rack on which hung keys of all kinds, among which were ignition keys.

The starter whirred for a full minute before the cold motor fired, and Curly revved the engine to peak for another minute to get it warmed up. The roar made Nels Larssen very anxious, and he approached Ted with a warning:

"Are we not taking a big risk . . . with all this noise ?"

Ted shook his head and laughed.

"You start trying to creep about when you are on a stunt like this, Mr. Larssen . . . and you arouse suspicion. Bang about, make a noise, and the folks take it for granted everything is right."

"One thing, Sergeant," the Norwegian said apologetically. "I wish you would not call me Mister. I am Nels to my friends."

"Nels, eh ? Okay, Nels it'll be. I've decided you're on our side," and he thrust out a gloved hand.

They piled into the lorry, Nels Larssen sitting next to the German and obeying instructions by slipping the hand grenade into the officer's left hand coat pocket, and keeping his own hand there as well. It was just a gentle hint of what the German could expect if he tried any treachery. Curly let in the clutch with a clashing of gears, and a few moments later they were crunching over the snow, the headlights full on, and lighting up the houses and the piles of snow on either side of the narrow street.

In the attic of the headquarters the Germans had waited in silence until they heard the engine start. When they heard the lorry drive away there was immediate activity. Three of the huskiest men formed themselves into a human battering ram, and within thirty seconds the pinewood planks of the door had given way.

Kapitan Schloss raced down the stairs, holding up his trousers with his left hand, his right hand on the stair rail. He dashed into the Orderly Room and picked up a telephone. The moment he clapped it to his ear he knew what had happened, for the line was dead.

One thing had been overlooked, however. In a corner was a wall telephone which had a direct line to a road-block about a mile from the village. Schloss cranked the handle furiously, swearing to himself when there was a delay in getting an answer.

"*Achtung!*" he bellowed when a voice asked what he wanted. "A lorry is coming your way. The Commanding Officer is in it—a prisoner. The men in the lorry are British Commando troops. Put your road-block down. That lorry must not get through. Understand . . . the lorry must not get through!"

"The lorry has just passed," came the apologetic, almost frightened reply. "The Commanding Officer gave us the password. We . . ."

"Oh, you fool. Couldn't you see that the men were British ?" Schloss raved. Then, realising he was wasting time. "Follow the lorry. Get word down the road to other posts. The lorry must not get away. You will go to the railway siding . . . they may try to get away by train. Stop them whatever the cost."

There was a click as the receiver at the other end was hung up, and Schloss blew out a great sigh, then felt for a cigarette. If the British got away there would be lots of trouble, and he would be in the middle of it. He shivered as he thought of the Commanding Officer. What that man could do to him would make anyone shiver. It was quite on the cards that he would have Schloss posted to the Russian front.

Ten minutes later, while his men were outside looking for the missing belts, boots and braces, the telephone bell rang sharply.

"Kapitan Schloss here . . . what news ?"

"We are engaging the Britishers at the railway siding; we are afraid to get too close in case we hit the Commanding Officer."

Schloss thought for a moment, then snapped:

"You have got to stop those men . . . no matter what the risk. Get close and kill or capture them all. Understand . . . kill or capture every man."

CHAPTER FOUR

BESIEGED

CURLY drove the lorry off the road towards the gates of the railway siding, his headlights full on. There was no sign of a sentry, but when they were some thirty yards from the gates there were two spurts of flame, and the windscreen was shattered into fragments. Curly stiffened, and his foot went down on the accelerator even more, so that the engine thundered uproariously.

The two rifles spat flame once more, and the German officer sitting next to Curly gave a little jerk, then slumped forward, and would have slid off the seat if Nels Larssen had not grabbed him.

Tat-tat-tat-tat-tat! Ted Harris had not relaxed, even though everything seemed to be going smoothly, and he had been watching events from the back of the lorry, peering along the side, and held in position by Sam Foster. His tommy-gun belched flame and lead, and he had the satisfaction of seeing a helmeted figure pitch forward into the glare of the headlights even as the second sentry fired again.

A moment later the lorry smashed into the big gates. There was a thunderous cracking as timbers smashed. The lorry heaved as the back wheels skidded for a moment, then gripped and sent the vehicle surging on.

The second sentry, already running for shelter went down to a short burst of fire from China Brown.

"Everybody all right ?" Ted called, now peering over the back of the lorry towards the shattered gates, his finger on the trigger, ready to send another burst of lead if any Germans were left behind them.

"I've copped one," Curly called. "I'm stopping . . . now . . . before . . ." The lorry came to an abrupt halt as Curly's foot went hard down on the brake pedal, killing the engine, and leaving them in a silence which wrapped about them like a thick blanket.

Curly was lifted from the wheel. He was faint, and only keeping his wits by biting on his lower lip. The bullet had smashed his right arm above the elbow. When they lifted the German out he was past attention.

"Not bad shooting," China murmured. "They'd got guts to stand up when we were belting at them."

"Sam . . . get down to the gateway, and hold off anyone else who comes. It looks to me as if somebody has managed to get a telephone working. These guards must have been warned. Nels . . . where are the Diesel engines kept? It's going to be touch and go."

"Have I to stop down there?" Sam asked, carefully putting a full magazine in his tommy-gun.

"Pull back if the Jerries come and it gets too hot," Ted ordered. "If we get out . . . we all get out. We're not leaving any rearguard to be taken prisoner."

Sam nodded and gave a little sigh of relief. He would have stayed behind if ordered, but he felt better to think he would be getting out with the others . . . if there was any getting out.

Down at the gate he flicked on his torch and looked at the two German guards. One appeared to be dead, the other was merely wounded. Sam pulled him to one side and made him as comfortable as he could.

"*Englischen?*" the soldier asked.

"That's right," Sam agreed. "How are you feeling, chum? Sorry we'd to knock you out."

"Sorry . . ." The wounded German gave a little grunt of astonishment, then shook his head. "I live in England for some time . . . Manchester. You know Manchester?"

"Not much," Sam had to admit. "Curly comes

from somewhere near that place. I live in a village . . . work on a farm, in peace-time."

"Better that you surrender," the German said after a slight pause. "The news has been passed on. We received telephone message a minute back. Passed news on down the line. Road blocks all manned. Bridges on railway guarded. Better surrender and live."

"Thanks for the tip," Sam said, and feeling in his pocket brought out part of a block of chocolate. "Here, have a chew. Sorry I haven't got the full block. Ate some a bit back."

The German took the chocolate, but his hand was shaking and he dropped the half block into the snow. Sam bent to retrieve it, and as he did so his ears caught a distant roar . . . a lorry was approaching.

"Here, chum, let me haul you out of the way. There's trouble coming. Don't want you getting shot by your own pals."

He dragged the German aside, placing him some dozen yards from the gateway then rushed back just as the approaching lorry left the road and turned in towards the siding gate.

The Germans were driving without lights, but Sam could see the dark bulk of the vehicle. He lifted his tommy-gun and squeezed the trigger.

"Tat-tat-tat-tat-tat-tat-tat-tat."

The night was suddenly hideous with the

spluttering rattle of automatic fire, and the snow was lit up with the flashes from the gun. From the direction of the lorry came the crash of shattering glass and the yelps of wounded men. The lorry turned sharply, and came to a sudden shuddering halt with its front wheels in a ditch.

Sam did not stay in the spot from which he had fired. He leapt like a gazelle to one side, and the next burst of fire came from a dozen yards away. It was just as well that he had moved, for two automatic weapons on the German side came into action, pouring lead in withering spray over the ground where Sam had been standing only a few moments earlier.

Sam stopped the guns with a very brief burst of fire, and even as he eased his finger off the trigger he was throwing himself down on the snow. There was a burst of fire from another automatic weapon, and the bullets went over Sam like a swarm of angry bees, one plucking at his woollen cap and making him cringe.

"Cor, that nearly parted my hair," he murmured, and replied with a third short burst.

By now the unwounded Germans had all left the truck, and were spreading out. There were several shots fired at Sam by riflemen, but he was not there. One of the earliest tricks he had been taught was never to stay in the same place during this kind of close-quarter work. Fire and fizzle off, had been Ted's injunction, and though Sam took longer than others to learn a lesson, he never forgot what he learned.

The night was filled now with sudden bursts of fire, and occasional rifle shots as the Germans blazed away into the darkness, hoping by a lucky shot to get some of the British Commandos they thought were holding the gateway. They were not anxious to advance, for they did not know how many men they were up against, and the fact that they had already been fired at from three different points kept them cautious.

The arrival of another lorry, however, altered the situation. Someone threw a hand grenade. It was many yards off the target, but the pieces of hot bomb-casing whined through the air far too close to Sam for comfort.

Rising to his feet he raced for the shelter of the nearest railway truck, and having put another magazine in his tommy-gun, he loosed off a short burst, then lifted himself off the ground. It was cool, clever work, for the Germans were no fools, and they fired low down, knowing that the trucks, which were of metal, would shield the body, but that a bullet in the leg would bring the strongest man down.

An officer had arrived with the second truck, and he began to give orders.

"Time I wasn't here," Sam murmured, and

sprinted farther into the siding. Where his friends were he did not know, nor did he know what they were doing; but he had to find them. He knew Ted's ideas were of commandeering a Diesel engine and making a run down the line for the coast. It was a plan they would have to abandon now if the alarm had been given all down the road, and, probably, all down the line.

As he ran he heard China Brown yelling to him:

"Sam . . . Sam . . . come on, pick up thy musket, we're going to miss the last train."

Sam could not run faster, and now bullets were whining about, flattening as they struck the metal trucks, and ricocheting through the air. Sam hated ricochets : the flattened bullets, which screamed mournfully about, were more dangerous than a direct shot. A ricochet could go in almost any direction, and because the bullet was knocked out of shape a wound was deadly.

"This way . . . this way," China was yelling, and as Sam hared over the beaten snow he could hear the thumming of a powerful Diesel engine.

A moment or so later he saw a pin-point of light: a masked torch in the hands of Ted Harris. Sam changed direction, and reached his friends. There was a truck coupled to the Diesel, and in it were Nels Larssen and Curly. Ted was going to drive the Diesel. Sam's job was to be in the cab with him to keep an eye on the line ahead, and give covering fire as they left the sidings.

"Can't do it," Sam gasped. "Spoke to one of the wounded Jerries at the gate. The alarm's been given all down the line. They'll be watching the line."

"What's been happening?" Ted's coolness had its effect on Sam, who pulled himself together with an effort. He gave a quick report about the arrival of two truck-loads of Germans, and finished:

"It isn't any use trying to get away by train . . . the line will be watched. They could derail us easy as winking."

"Hear that," Ted called. "What do you think?"

"I'm willing to chance my arm," the reply came from Curly, and was followed almost immediately by a scoffing:

"Chance *your* arm, you clot. You've already got a bullet in one. Do you want both out of action?" Then, more seriously, China continued: "I'm willing to do what you want, Sarge. It looks like heads we lose, tails the Jerries win. If we go out by rail we'll be ditched. If we stop here we haven't the chance of a paper cat in a burning barn. They'll get us before daylight."

"We'll go out," Ted said. "Sam . . . know anything about Diesel engines?"

"Sorry, Sarge," and Sam shook his head.

"All right, uncouple the truck. Nels . . . get Curly out. China, I'm leaving you to hold the fort. We're going to draw the Jerries off."

"Who do you mean . . . *we?*"

"Me and Sam," was the curt retort. "Come on, Sam . . . we've got to kid 'em that we're all making a dash for it. On second thoughts we won't uncouple the truck. You stay in the truck, Sam . . . give the Jerries everything we've got . . . grenades, tommy-gun bursts. I'll see to the engine driving."

Curly was helped out of the truck. His wound had been hastily bandaged with a first field dressing, and the bandage was already stained red. Curly was tough, but his face was pale. That wound put him right out of any chance of fighting. He swayed as they stood him on his feet for a moment. He needed a doctor.

"Hide as best you can, China," Ted ordered. "Me and Sam will be back as soon as we can. I'm leaving you in charge."

"Promoted, you mean ?" China asked, a chuckle in his voice. "What am I getting, one stripe or two?"

There was no time for further talk. The silence which hung over the small railway sidings was ominous. It suggested that the Germans were making a quiet search, and every moment lost now made the chance of discovery more certain.

Even as Ted stepped into the cab of the Diesel engine there was a sudden burst of automatic fire, and the bullets splattered about the brick-work of the building, knocking off chips, and sending dust flying about.

"Ready, Sam?"

"Ready, Sarge." Sam had collected three hand grenades from China, he had three spare maga-zines for his tommy-gun, and he could have done with a drink. Sam's throat felt dry as cotton-wool. He knew what would happen the moment Ted started the Diesel out into the open. There would be concentrated fire on to it.

Climbing into the steel truck he laid his tommy-gun at his feet, making sure it was cocked and that the safety-catch was "off." He put one grenade in his left pocket, and one in the right, keeping one in his right hand. He slipped a thumb into the split-pin ring, and gently pulled out the safety-pin.

"Okay, see you later, lads. We won't be too long. I'll whistle ' Lily Marlene ' when we come back," and with that promise Ted started the Diesel moving forward.

There was no concealing the fact that they were moving, for right at the entrance to the building there were cross-over points which clanked under the wheels.

At once there were winking points of fire from

several directions, and the chattering roar of automatic weapons.

"Tac-a-tac-a-tac-a-tac-a-tac-atac." Followed almost at once by the bellowing: "Tung-tung-tung-tung-tung-tung" of bullets smashing into the steel-sided trucks, and against the metal-work of the Diesel engine. Sparks flew in all directions, and bullets ricocheted here and there, moaning and whining as ricocheting bullets will. It seemed utter madness for anyone to show even an eyelash, yet Sam swung his right arm back, released the firing lever on the bomb, counted two, then flung it into the air.

Then he ducked as low as he could.

The bomb rose some thirty feet, began to fall, and exploded with a vicious "Crang!"

Every gun stopped, and there were two yells of anguish as pieces of grenade shrapnel put at least two Germans out of the fight.

The Diesel began to pick up speed, the fish-plates on the narrow gauge rails clattering mournfully from want of attention. There was no camouflaging where the one-truck train was, and after a few seconds the barrage of automatic fire began again, the flashes of fire winking in and out with unbelievable speed from several points as the Germans ran along the siding, firing whenever they came to a suitable point.

Sam stood up, waited, even though bullets

were whining and moaning past him, as well as smacking against the truck side. Then he opened up. A short quick burst at one winking gun muzzle; a quick switch of aim, and an equally short burst at another gunner.

His own weapon was flashing fire, making him a target for anyone quick enough to turn a gun on him. Sam ducked down as four guns sent a hail of lead at him. He could feel the bullets thudding against the truck side. One or two actually ripped small holes in the metal, and the battered bullets fell into the trucks.

Now the Germans were firing from the rear, for the Diesel was doing some twenty miles an hour under full throttle, and beginning to run out of the long lines of trucks which cluttered the siding. Sam risked another two quick bursts, and lost his woollen cap. It was as if a passing bird had laid a claw on it and flown on. The woolly just sailed off into the night. Sam licked his dry lips. Then bent low, flicked on his torch, and picked up the cap. It had been thrown to the other end of the truck. The little white button which formed the centre of the cap had been split in two.

"Sam, you're lucky," he murmured and drew the cap on again. The cold was so intense there was a risk of frostbite to the ears without a woolly to cover them.

For a mile and a half the Diesel raced along, the countryside completely shrouded in darkness. Nor were there any signal lights. The beating of the fishplates under the wheels began to increase and the truck to sway from side to side. It was a narrow-gauge railway, and not meant for light engines to race over.

Sam began to wish Ted would close his throttle a little. Then, quite suddenly, he was sliding towards the front of the truck as the brakes were applied. Sparks flew in all directions and not only the engine but the truck bumped and shuddered as if meaning to leave the rails.

"Come on, Sam." Ted's crisp command was like music in Sam's ears. If there was one thing he wanted to do more than another at that moment it was to "come on" out of the truck.

As the wheels gave a last groan under the grip of the brake shoes Sam leapt over the side, and grunted as his feet hit the track. There was snow there, but Sam was no baby-weight, and his feet dug deep even in the hard-packed frozen mantle.

"Where are you, Sarge?" he asked, looking round in vain for Ted.

"Be with you in a tick," Ted assured him, and even as he spoke the truck and the Diesel engine began to move forward. The engine racing for a few seconds as the wheels spun wildly before gripping the rails again.

Then Ted was coming along the track. He was grinning.

"Reckon you were like me, Sam . . . got through without a scratch."

"I thought I'd lost my woollen cap," Sam said soberly. "Had it whipped right off my head. The button at the top is cut clean in two."

"You'll have to get that mended before the next kit inspection," Ted chaffed. "Or you'll be on the hooks for damaging your equipment. Lor, I could just do with a cig."

"I've got some." Sam dug his hand into his trousers' pocket, but Ted stopped him.

"No time, now, Sam." He stood watching the train vanish into the night a blurred shape swallowed up in moments, except for the steadily rising clatter of wheels going over rail joints. "I ought to have switched the lights on, Sam. I wonder how far she'll run before they derail. They'll have a bit of a disappointment when they start searching the wreckage for bodies."

"I wonder how Curly's feeling," Sam whispered. "I wish it hadn't been him. He's so useful."

"Useful!" Ted growled. "What do you mean . . . 'he's so useful'? China's useful. You're useful."

"Yes, but Curly's . . . well, Curly's different. He doesn't get scared so easy. Not like me."

"Sam, I scare. I dare say Curly scares, too. Anybody who doesn't get scared when bullets are flying about isn't human. Know why I picked you to come with me?"

"I dunno. Except I suppose that you wouldn't have liked to leave me with Curly. It wouldn't have been right. . . . I mean he needs somebody proper to look after him."

Sergeant Ted Harris stood for a moment staring at the dimly-seen figure of Sam, then he laid a hand on his comrade's shoulder, opened his mouth as if to say something, then decided to leave it unsaid. He clapped Sam on the back, then turned north again for the siding they had just left. It was no use telling Sam he had been chosen for this operation "Lightning" because he had already proved more than once that he had everything that a Commando needs, strength, quick action with weapons, steady courage, and a loyalty beyond telling. Sam would have thought Ted was pulling his leg.

They climbed up on to the low embankment, Ted assuring Sam that their white clothing would keep them invisible, and yet from that height they ought to be able to see if any Germans in their darker uniforms were moving about.

When they drew near the marshalling yard they stopped and listened. It was Sam who thought he heard voices, and they had crept another fifty yards on before Ted heard the murmur. Then they saw the pink spots of light which were cigarettes.

"We could put the lot of 'em down with a couple of bursts," Ted whispered. "But we won't."

"Shall I go to the shed where we left Curly and China ?" Sam asked.

"We'll both go."

They moved like shadows. When they were passing the dark metal trucks they bent low, so that their white dress would not show against the dark background.

Instead of making for the big doors of the shed where they had left their two comrades and Nels Larssen, they went to the back, and Ted began to whistle very softly the German war tune "Lily Marlene":

"Underneath the lamplight, by the barrack gate . . ."

It was a haunting tune, sung and whistled not only by Rommel's men in the western desert, but by the British Desert Rats, by Germans in Norway and in the bitter wastes of Russia.

When Ted ceased his whistling he and Sam waited in silence. There was no answering whistle, and Sam felt his throat tighten a little. That silence suggested Curly, China and Nels Larssen had been found and captured. Perhaps they were already dead.

"China wouldn't surrender until he'd finished his last round, and his last grenade," Sam said soberly. "And Curly couldn't fight. He'll be suffering from shock."

"Go on, Sam, pile it on," Ted muttered grimly. "Larssen couldn't fight because I wouldn't let him carry a gun."

"I didn't understand the reason for that," Sam whispered. "He looks a handy sort of chap, and I think he's got courage."

"He's not in uniform," Ted explained. "If Jerry catches us we do stand a bit of a chance . . . even if Hitler has said we're all to be shot at once. We're here as soldiers. Larssen, being a civvy, could be shot out of hand as a member of the Underground Movement, or even as a spy."

There was a short silence, then Sam asked:

"What are we going to do now, Sarge?" The words seemed to stick in his throat, and he was half afraid that Sergeant Harris would say they must make for the coast. Down there, where the fjord opened out into the sea a submarine would surface in seventy-two hours. A collapsible boat would be rowed ashore, if the sub's signals were answered. Members of "Operation Lightning" who had managed to reach the rendezvous in time would be taken aboard the submarine, and a day or so later would be landed in Scotland.

"There shouldn't be any difficulty getting down

to the coast," Ted said, half to himself. "There's far more night than day at this time of the year, and if we couldn't dodge the Jerries we'd deserve all we got."

"You mean we're leaving Curly and China?" There was something like horror in Sam's voice. "Suppose you went . . . and reported at the submarine. I'd wait here, and . . ." he shrugged, then said pleadingly. "Couldn't we wait a bit, Sarge? I mean . . . it doesn't seem fair to leave China and Curly, specially now that Curly's wounded."

"You're a funny cove, Sam," Ted replied. "I never said we were leaving them. I'm waiting until that bunch of Jerries moves off. You make yourself comfortable, Sam. Have a snooze if you like. I'll keep watch."

Ten minutes passed, then there came the sound of a lorry arriving. The Germans stubbed out their cigarettes, clambered aboard, and within another three minutes the railway siding was wrapped in silence.

"We'd best make sure if they've left a guard," Ted decided, "then if . . ." He stopped, for a low whistle was heard, coming from the darkness somewhere behind them, a familiar tune, too, the first line of a verse of "Lily Marlene," the popular soldiers' song.

Within a minute Sam and Ted had rejoined

China, Larssen, and Curly who was squatting in the snow.

"We'd to beat it quick," China explained. "The Jerries were all over the place, and but for Nels, here, me and Curly would have been sunk. Curly passed out. Y'know, Ted . . ."

"Sergeant!" Ted suggested.

"Sorry . . . y'know—*Sergeant Harris*, I think we'll have to get Curly to a doctor. That arm's bleeding bad. Don't seem to slow down at all. I'm scared he's going to bleed to death. I think the bullet must have slashed an artery."

"What about putting a tourniquet on?" Sam suggested. "I don't know how it's done . . . but it'll stop any sort of bleeding."

"We'll get him to a doctor," Ted decided, and turning to the silent Norwegian he asked: "Nels, is there a doctor in the village? A Norwegian doctor?"

Nels Larssen seemed not to have heard the question and Ted was about to repeat it when the Norwegian shrugged.

"There is a doctor," he admitted; "but how can you get attention for wounded Curly? Doctor's house is in village. He dare not come here . . . you could not get there," and he spread his hands in a gesture of helplessness.

"Look, Nels, I agreed to take you back with us to England," Ted pointed out. "If I go back I

take Curly with me. If I don't go back . . .
what's going to happen to you ? I don't want to
get tough with you . . . but I'm going to get
Curly to a doctor. What about it ? Are you going
to show me the way ?"

"Give me a gun," Nels spoke in a voice that
was suddenly crisp. "Why should I not have
arms ? I am Norwegian. My country is at war.
If I am taken prisoner I die. So . . . I might as
well take some Germans with me. Give me a
gun and I will take you to the doctor's house."

Ted drew a .38 Smith and Wesson.

"It's loaded in all five chambers. Here are
three packets of ammo. China, give me a hand.
I'll get Curly on my back. No use wasting time."

Then Curly spoke. His voice was weak and
shaky.

"I'm not coming," he croaked. "Y'know the
orders . . . leave the wounded. You can't do
nothing for me. If you try you'll all get it in the
neck. The Jerries won't waste time on a trial.
Beat it, Sarge, and good luck."

"Curly, I happen to be the sergeant of this out-
fit," Ted's voice was low and gentle. "So *I'll* give
the orders. We're taking you to a doctor."

"You're a fool, Ted Harris," Curly whispered;
opened his mouth to say something else, only to
close his eyes as he fainted again.

Curly was no lightweight, and Ted staggered

a little until he had got the wounded man balanced over his shoulder in a "fireman's" lift. Then, with a little grunt as he shaped to start across the frozen snow, he said:

"China . . . while I'm carrying Curly, you'll take the lead."

"Promoted again, eh ?" China said, "well, well, I always wanted stripes. Sam . . . bring up the rear, and don't shoot till I start."

They moved round the back of the deserted engine-house, four vague shadows in the darkness. Their ears were strained to catch the slightest sound, but they heard nothing.

China scouted ahead, and returned to say there was no one at the wrecked gates. The lorry which had run into the ditch when Sam fired a burst through the windscreen was still there and would take a lot of moving. China thought the front axle was broken.

Three times during the first ten minutes' walk up the road they had to throw themselves into the piled snow at the roadside as first a motor cyclist, then a car, and finally a lorry-load of troops raced by, heading south.

"Must think we're down the road," Sam suggested. Ted did not reply. He was grunting at every step, now, for Curly was heavy. China relieved him, then Sam relieved China.

They went off the road to by-pass the road-block, and could have shot down the guards there with no trouble at all if they had wished. By the time they reached the first of the wooden houses even Nels had taken a turn at carrying Curly, and they were all tiring.

"How far up the village, Nels?" Ted asked, and had difficulty in hiding his dismay when the Norwegian said soberly:

"Four doors only from German headquarters. Better not to try it. It is too dangerous."

Ted masked his torch and let the thin beam shine on Curly's face. It was pale, and there was hardly any colour in his lips. Unless he had medical attention quickly he would be dead before daylight.

"Step on it, lads," he said, heaving Curly to an upright position, then allowing him to slump over his right shoulder. "It's a doctor . . . or bust. Are you with me ?"

"Hear that, Sam ?" China murmured, taking out the last hand grenade of his stock. "He's *asking* us . . . not telling us." Then in a brisker voice: "Carry on, Sergeant Harris . . . we're with you."

"The drinks are on me when we get home," Ted puffed, and started up the road.

CHAPTER FIVE

LAMBS IN THE DEN
OF WOLVES

TED made no attempt to slink up the deserted road. He kept to the side, but not close to the houses, and marched as briskly as the heavy weight of Curly would allow.

Ahead they could hear the guttural voices of Germans outside the headquarters, and then the sound of a lorry starting up.

"This is it," China whispered, cocking his tommy-gun. "If they come down with their headlamps on we've had it."

"You haven't got a spare grenade, China, have you ?" Sam asked, a pleading note in his voice.

"I have one, and if I'd two I wouldn't let you have it," China made no bones about refusing Sam's request. "I'm the grenade expert . . . it says so on my regimental documents. Trained, I am. You're not."

With his tommy-gun under his left arm, the grenade in his right hand, pin out, he marched ahead of Ted, while the lorry, unseen as yet, roared and yowled as someone kept pushing down the accelerator pedal as far as it would go, revving the engine until it screamed at peak.

"Warming it up in a hurry," China said. "If they did that in our mob they'd be on the peg next morning . . . for ill-treating Government property."

"This way," Nels Larssen hissed, and indicated a big, dark, silent house just short of the square.

They were all tense as Nels tapped urgently on the thick wooden door. If the lorry came round the corner they would be seen, and now they were so near getting help for poor Curly they were all taut-nerved. For once they did not want a fight. All they wanted was to get Curly into the hands of a doctor.

Tap-tap-tap-tap-tap!

The tapping sounded as if it must echo through every room of the house, yet there was no reply.

"If we don't get Curly in soon it'll be too late," Ted snarled, "if the Germans weren't so close I'd risk a shot through the lock. Are you sure he's at home, Larssen?"

The Norwegian shrugged.

"Maybe he is called out to attend to German wounded," he suggested. "If that is so . . . well!" and he shrugged again.

"Sarge," it was Sam. "What about the V-sign?"

"The V-sign?" Ted was both worried and tired, and for a moment he did not realise what Sam was suggesting.

"You know . . . the Churchill V-sign. It's Morse. V for Victory," Sam was beginning to sound enthusiastic. "Maybe if you tapped three times then scraped the muzzle of a gun on the door for the dash in the morse, the doctor would realise we were friends."

Nels Larssen's eyes lit up.

"Yes, try it, sergeant. I have an idea. The doctor may not come because we do not knock loud enough. If it is the German who knocks . . . he beats on the door with a revolver, or the butt of a gun. So . . . Doctor Lorensen may be uneasy, wondering who we are."

"But any ordinary doctor would answer a knock," Ted protested.

"No doctor is ordinary . . . when Germans occupy the village," Larssen said quietly. "Shall I try the V-sign?"

"Try anything so long as we get Curly somewhere proper where his wound can be seen to."

The V-sign was made. Three sharp taps, then a scraping along the planking of the door with the muzzle of the Smith and Wesson revolver. All the time the three Britishers were listening to the voices of the Germans who seemed to be arguing as to who boarded the lorry, the engine of which had now settled down to a steady tick-over purring.

"We should have gone to the back door," Sam muttered, "why didn't we think of that at first."

"We cannot use the doctor's back door," Nels Larssen said patiently as he knocked three times and then scraped his gun muzzle again. "The doctor's back door is locked and sealed. The Germans wish to make sure that if any man is injured he cannot be treated under cover. There have been one or two men hurt . . . there *are* some Norwegian patriots who still fight the Germans."

"Sorry, didn't mean to . . ." Sam began, then stopped. There had been a scraping of a bolt behind the door, and now there was a widening black gap. Who was behind it could not be seen, but Ted Harris did not wait for an invitation to enter. He strode into the house, followed by the other three, and barely had the door been closed than the sound of the lorry was heard, and as it rolled down the narrow street the timbering of the house vibrated.

"Phew . . . that's what you might call a narrow squeak, Sam," China whispered, then went into a back room on Ted Harris's heels.

The doctor turned up an oil-lamp, took one quick look at the white anoraks, the tommy-guns, then indicated a couch on to which Curly could be laid.

The hours that followed were long and anxious. Curly had lost a lot of blood. The doctor's room was not properly fitted to give a blood trans-fusion, but he did it. Sam gave a pint of blood, as did Ted Harris. China's blood was not the right blood group, so his offer of a "pint or two," as he put it, was turned down.

In the cellar the doctor's buxom wife provided blankets, and right in the heart of the German-occupied village the Commandos lay down and slept. They were sleeping when the doctor's wife brought hot drinks, and with a nod of her head she took the drinks away. They could be given later. At the moment the Britishers needed sleep more than anything else.

It was the end of the next day, though only just past three in the afternoon, when Ted Harris was wakened by a touch from Larssen. The Norwegian was pale faced even in the lamp-light.

"The doctor's wife has just been in," Nels said urgently. "The Germans are beginning to think you are here in the village. They plan a thorough search of every house. If we stay here it will mean death for the doctor. He will be sent to a con-centration camp, or shot for harbouring us."

Ted woke the others, and they went quietly

up the stairs to the back room where Curly had been given his blood transfusions. He was no longer there. Now a table was drawn up against the couch, and there was food ready.

It was a silent group who ate the simple meal. In the darkness they might be able to get out of the house unseen; but there was no hope of getting the wounded Curly out.

The doctor's wife, with Nels acting as interpreter, said her husband would be back soon, and would give them the latest news.

"I don't like the idea of leaving Curly," China muttered gloomily. "It doesn't seem right. What do you think, Sam?"

Sam shrugged.

"I think what Sergeant Harris thinks," he said, and there was the hint of a twinkle in his eyes.

"Why, you don't know what he thinks," China spluttered. "He's just sitting there like a brass Buddha. Saying nothin', seeing nothin', hearing nothin'. How can you think the same as him?"

Sam shrugged again and grinned.

"If I think we ought to stay, and Sarge thinks we ought to go . . . I'll just have to think the same way as him, so what."

"That's sense, Sam." Ted's face lost some of its seriousness for a moment.

"It ain't sense," China grumbled. "It's the old Army motto of: ' Don't do what you think . . .

do what you're told. You aren't paid to think.'
A daft idea, anyway."

"I think I'd better find you blokes something
to do," Ted told them. "Sam, I don't suppose
your tommy-gun would be worse for cleaning,
would it ? The same goes for you, China. I'll
clean my own . . . and Curly's."

They were reassembling their weapons when the
doctor arrived. He was tall, fair-haired, a typical
Viking type, now they could get a good look at
him. He nodded and smiled as Nels introduced
them. There had been neither the time nor the
inclination to talk during the blood transfusions
the previous night.

Through Nels he told them the latest news.
The Diesel engine and truck had been derailed
some five miles down the line, and the Germans
had been amazed when they could find no bodies.
They had inspected the railway sidings as soon
as it was light, and had tried tracker dogs after
finding bloodstains on the snow near the lorry
the Britishers had abandoned.

Captain Schloss, who was in command for the
time being, after the death of the Garrison
Commander, shot by the German sentry while he
sat by Curly's side in the lorry, had decided to
search every house in the neighbourhood.

"He thinks you must be hiding in some farm-
house. The farms are being searched now,"

Nels Larssen translated. "To-morrow, if you have not been found, the houses in the village will be searched. A notice has been pinned up offering a reward for information about you, and also threatening death to anyone who hides you."

Ted sucked hard at his cigarette.

"Looks as if we're in a bit of a jam, chaps. Point is . . . we can't leave Curly here, or it means trouble for the doctor and his family. Here, Nels, ask the doctor how soon Curly could be moved."

There was a quick exchange of Norwegian, then Nels, his face grave, said:

"The wound is clean, and should begin healing almost at once; but he is too weak to move. Two days, three days, and he might be able to walk. Until then . . ." and Nels shrugged.

Ted drew deep on his cigarette, then nipping out the glowing end pushed the butt into a small pocket. He might need a puff or two later on, and a stub would be useful.

"We can't leave the doctor to carry the can, chaps," he said gravely. "Yet we can't get Curly away. Any ideas ?"

"Sounds like that old puzzle," China commented: "You know the one—Which came first, the hen or the egg ?—I don't know the answer to that puzzle, and I can't see any answer to your question, Sarge. What *can* we do ?"

They sat in silence for the better part of ten minutes, then the grim lines about Ted's mouth slowly smoothed away. The corners of his mouth creased a little, and Sam Foster's eyes lit up when he realised the sergeant was actually grinning.

" Got an idea, Sarge ?"

"Yes. Nels . . . can we get out of here, unseen ? Ask the doctor. Could we climb over the house roof, for instance ? I daresay there'll be Germans in the streets if they're thinking of starting a house-to-house search."

There followed a conversation between Nels and the doctor, then the Norwegian turned to Ted.

"It will be difficult, and dangerous," he began. "There is snow on the roof-tops; but you can get out that way through a skylight in the top room. The doctor asks what you propose to do."

"We're going to draw a herring across the trail," Ted said, and decided he would treat himself to another smoke. He brought out his cigarette stub and got a light from Sam. "You don't know what drawing a herring across the trail means ? A red herring, they say in England."

Nels shook his head.

"I know what a herring is, to be sure. A red herring I do not know. Is it one that has been smoked ?"

"I don't mean a real herring," Ted explained.

"To draw a red herring across the trail is a way of saying you are laying a false trail. If we can kid the Germans into believing we are nowhere near this village, then they won't waste time searching the houses. That means Curly would be safe, as well as Doctor Sorensen and his family. What do you think?"

Nels frowned, then shrugged.

"It will be very dangerous for you," he suggested. "You will be on the run all the time. The Germans will comb the district. Where will you get food. Where will you sleep?"

"We'll think about that later," Ted chuckled. "Nels, Commandos are trained to be tough. All right . . . this is one time when we've got to be tough, eh, Sam?"

Sam Foster nodded.

An hour later, with as much food in their pockets as the doctor's wife could spare, they went up to the attic. Darkness shrouded everything, and even when the black-out cloth had been removed from the attic window no light came in. There was a low cloud ceiling which masked the stars.

"Couldn't be better, Sarge," China suggested. "We . . . ow, right down my neck."

The doctor had managed to force up the attic skylight, and a cloud of powdery snow drifted down. He apologised, and China grinned.

"Forget it. I dessay there'll be more cussing about snow down my neck before this jaunt's finished."

One by one they were helped up on to the snow-covered roof. They shook hands with the doctor, with Nels, then the skylight was lowered back in place, and they might have been on the roof of the world, for all the signs of life they could see.

There was about an inch of powdery snow, the result of a slight fall during the morning. Underneath that the surface was crisp, and it crunched beneath their feet as they edged their way along the roof-top towards the end of the short row of houses.

Twenty minutes later they were on the street, having made a perilous descent by means of a drain pipe. Their hands were stiff with cold, for they had been forced to take off their gloves in order to grip the pipe, and they stood in a corner flexing their fingers.

"We've got to strike quickly," Ted whispered, "and draw the Jerries away from the village. How much ammo. have we, Sam?"

Their ammunition was low. Between them they had two and a half magazines, and one hand grenade.

"We'll have to use Jerry ammo., that's all," Ted decided. "I think they use .300 stuff, and that'll suit us fine."

Like phantoms they slipped out of the village, keeping low between the walls of the houses and the banked snow from the roadway. Once a motor cyclist raced out of the night, going up towards the German headquarters, his head-lamp cutting a silvery swathe through the darkness. He saw nothing unusual for the three Britishers were lying flat, having dropped down the moment they heard the roar of his engine.

By-passing the first road-block Ted led his two men towards the siding. The gates had not been repaired, but there was a pink glow from a brazier.

"I don't think we'll touch this bunch," Ted decided. "The farther away from the village we get the better. I expect there'll be another road-block farther down."

They had to walk nearly five miles before they came to another road-block and this one guarded the entrance to a hamlet of scattered houses. There was a small hut, a fire, and a stout larch-pole which could be swung down across the road to stop any vehicle.

A German soldier stood by the brazier, alternately warming first one cold hand, then the other, switching his rifle to do so. There was no lounging.

"They're on the alert," Ted mused. "So we'll have to get him . . . and any others in the hut.

You'll take the sentry, Sam; don't hurt him unless you have to. I'll give you the whistle when we're going in . . . from the far side, so the sentry will probably turn in that direction. Okay, Sam ?"

"Okay, Sarge."

Ted Harris might have been ordering Sam to blanco a belt, or do something equally harmless for all the emotion Sam showed. He strapped his tommy-gun across his shoulders where it would be out of the way, then moved to the road-side after Ted and China had melted into the night.

The sentry poked the coke burning in the brazier and it glowed a little brighter, revealing the German in his jackboots, heavy topcoat, oval scuttle steel-helmet over the top of a woollen balaclava-type helmet which kept his ears, throat and chin warm.

Sam moved nearer, as quietly as a cat stalking a sparrow, moving along on hands and knees until he was lying in the shallow ditch to one side of the sentry box not more than eight feet from the man.

Muscles tense, and expecting to hear Ted's signal whistle any moment, Sam pricked up his ears at the sound of an approaching lorry. The sentry cocked his head and lifted one side of his balaclava helmet for a moment, the better to hear. He then dropped the larch pole across the road and called to the hut a few yards to the rear.

Headlights lit up the road and the sentry clicked off his safety-catch as three other Germans raced out to join him, two privates and an N.C.O. The N.C.O. swung an oil lamp to and fro, a signal for the lorry to halt.

With a squealing of brakes the vehicle pulled up a foot or so from the barrier and the driver leaned out, showing a pass of some kind. The N.C.O. examined it by the light of his lamp while another of the guard went to look in the back of the lorry.

Satisfied that the lorry did not contain any British Commandos the soldier called something to the N.C.O. who was handing back the driver's pass. At that moment Ted Harris stepped into the glow of the lamp, moving so noiselessly that the Germans were unaware of him until he gave a loud, throat-clearing cough.

At almost the same moment China Brown came up from the road a yard or so behind the lorry, beginning to whistle a tuneless version of "Lily Marlene," Sam leapt out of the ditch, where he had taken off his tommy-gun, and now held it at the ready.

The Germans seemed petrified. Slowly the N.C.O. allowed his right arm to droop, and with it the lamp. The piece of paper which he had been about to hand to the lorry driver fluttered soundlessly to the hard-packed snow.

"Anybody speak English?" Ted asked, and it was apparent at once that none of them did, for there were only dazed looks. "Hm. Pity. Well, we'll have to get along without a chat." Ted reached out and took the rifle from the nearest German, then nodded to the others in turn who laid their weapons down in the snow. The lorry driver might have been chewing a huge wad of gum, for his throat was working convulsively, and his fear showed also in the beads of perspiration which broke out on his upper lip, glistening in the light of the lamp.

"Into the shed," a jerk with his tommy-gun did more than words, and the Germans marched obediently off the road and into the small hut. A carefully screened lamp lit up two bunks, a table, and a small oil stove. There was a telephone in the corner.

"Tie 'em up," Ted ordered, and when Sam began to look for rope, added: "Never mind rope . . . their belts will do. Strap their arms behind."

"They'll get away, Sarge," Sam protested, and gaped when Ted grinned as he said:

"That's the idea, Sam. We want 'em to get away. They've got to raise the alarm. Isn't that what we've come out for . . . to get the Jerries chasing us ?"

Sam grunted, and began to strap the arms of the men with their belts. Then he turned to the lorry driver, but stopped when Ted Harris waved him away.

"Leave him, Sam. He's got to drive the lorry . . . south." Ted looked at his tommy-gun. The magazine was only half full, and it was the full extent of his ammunition. "How many spare mags have you got, Sam ?"

"Only the mag I have in," Sam replied. "I've been wondering if we could get hold of some of their ammo. Will it fit ?"

"I don't think so," Ted screwed up his face in a frown of concentration, trying to remember what instructors had said during lectures back home. "Nine-millimetre stuff . . . and generally rimless."

"Oh, rimless won't do," Sam murmured. "Pity we didn't bring those two-bob Sten guns. They took nine millimetre rimless, didn't they ?"

"What about these, Sarge ?" Sam asked, bringing from a corner three German submachine-guns of the Schmiesser type.

Ted hefted one and nodded approval. It was well-balanced, clean, and the sort of weapon he could handle. Motioning the lorry driver to take it he stuck his own tommy-gun in the man's back and indicated that he should demonstrate how the Schmiesser worked.

The Germans on the floor watched in silence while the lorry driver, beads of perspiration rolling down his face, showed how the magazines fit, how the safety-catch worked, and even how a jammed bullet could be extracted.

"You should have been an instructor, Fritz," Ted chuckled as he took the weapon, and taking the magazine from his own tommy-gun threw that useless weapon into a corner. "Just take note, Sam, honesty is the best policy, and we're not stealing guns. We leave our tommy-guns and take these Jerry pieces. We'll borrow their ammunition. . . ."

"I've just had a funny idea," Sam broke in, his face one huge grin. "We shan't even be stealing the ammo. If we run into trouble the Jerries get their bullets back, eh ?"

For a moment Ted stared, then nodded, his face creasing into a grin.

"You've got something there, Sam," he agreed. "They'll certainly get 'em back right enough— and if they want the cartridge cases, all they'll have to do will be to pick 'em up."

They emptied a box of magazines, and filled their pockets until the stout material sagged under the weight. Then Ted ordered the lorry driver out of the hut. China sat beside the man while he started his engine and turned the vehicle round on the icy road. Not until Ted and Sam were safely in the back, with Ted pushing the muzzle of a "borrowed" German rifle in the driver's spine did China hop out and join his two companions in the rear.

Pushing two boxes of vegetables to the front of the lorry Ted jammed the rifle there, so that the muzzle would poke round the side of the seat into the driver's ribs, and keep on poking with every lurch of the lorry. When he was satisfied it would remain like that he leaned over the driver and said:

"Okay, Fritz, we'll go," and pointed down the dark, snow-covered road. Then, turning to Sam and China, he jerked a thumb to the tailboard. Sam and China merely stared, not understanding what they were to do.

As the German started his engine again Ted said with exaggerated weariness:

"Don't you blokes ever use those solid pieces of bone sticking on top of your necks? You were given heads to think with, you clots. Get out . . . beat it. You don't think we're going with this lorry, do you? Somewhere down this road there'll be another road-block, and more Jerries. As soon as we get away from this hut you drop off. I'll do the same after a minute or so, and I'll wait for you. When you drop off start walking after us . . . till you catch me up."

Turning, he leaned over the frightened German again and snarled:

"Go on, get her rolling," and he pointed towards the accelerator. The German understood no English, but there was no mistaking that gesture. He got into first gear, slowly released his clutch pedal, and with a little shivering skid on the ice, the lorry began to move south. It must have been nightmarish work driving over those roads, and even more so with an unshaven, grim-faced Sergeant Commando poking a gun in his ribs, and breathing down his ear. The German was trembling as he slowly worked up speed.

Ted continued to lean over him for a matter of a hundred yards, by which time the speed of the lorry had crept up to sixteen or seventeen miles an hour, and was slowly increasing. Swift acceleration under such treacherous conditions was quite impossible, just as stopping quickly was equally risky.

"Faster," Ted ordered, and then pushing the German rifle forward a little so that it was poking into the driver's back, he scurried to the back of the truck, swung over the tailboard, let his feet slide along the frozen surface for a second or so, then let go.

He took several amazing giant strides in an effort to keep on his feet, but his balance was gone, and he suddenly let all his muscles relax and tried to curl himself into a loose ball as he went over with a thump which made his teeth rattle.

Down the road the German driver had half turned to protest to his captors that he dare not go farther, as there was another road-block. Then the moment he realised the terrifying British sergeant was no longer there he switched off his engine, still leaving it in gear, and began to brake.

Some fifty yards ahead of him a lamp waved wildly and a leather-lunged sergeant called on him to stop. There was no stopping the lorry, for the road was on a slight incline. The locked wheels just slid over the icy surface and the driver did the only thing possible—he dived from the cab.

Up the road Sergeant Ted Harris was trying to collect his scattered wits when the silence of the night was broken by the crackle of small arms fire. Followed a few seconds later by a crash which seemed to make the very air quiver.

"Hope the driver got clear," Ted growled as he picked himself up and began gingerly feeling at himself. Down the road there were yells, and a loud bell began to ring furiously.

Ted shook himself again, then turned back.

He had to contact Sam and China. The three met within forty seconds, for Sam and China were hurrying as quickly as the slippery, hard-packed snow would allow.

"What happened, Sarge ?" China asked. "You're not hurt, are you ?"

"Hurt!" Ted muttered ruefully, gently rubbing the seat of his trousers. "I don't suppose I'll sit down in comfort for months. Apart from that and a few broken ribs, maybe a fracture of my skull . . . I'm okay, as far as I can tell."

"What was the firing ?" Sam was listening to the clamour from down the road.

"I'll tell you when we're not pushed for time," Ted grunted. "At the moment we're due to do a disappearing act, or the Jerries will be here."

"If they've shot the lorry driver they won't know about us," China pointed out as he followed Sam off the road, with Ted bringing up the rear. "I don't see the reason for panicking . . . if they don't know about us they can't follow."

"I wish you'd use your loaf, China," Ted snapped. "You take size seven and a half in caps and you act like you've got the brain of a baby ant."

"Ants are very intelligent," Sam said, grinning.

"Yes, of course they are," Ted agreed. "I beg the pardon of all ants. China hasn't the brains of a dead duck. Can't you guess why I wouldn't let Sam tie-up those Jerry guards, you dim-wit ?"

"But he did tie them up," China protested. "He used their belts."

"Yes, and they'd be free within a couple of minutes," Ted jeered. "Did you happen to notice if their hut contained a telephone? Did you, Sam?"

"Yes, Sarge. I wondered why you were taking such a chance," Sam mused.

"Chance," Ted groaned in mock horror. "Oh, give me strength to put up with the pair of you. I wanted the Jerries to get free; I wanted them to raise the alarm by telephone. Wasn't that agreed, that we should kid the Jerry Command that we were not hiding in the village where Doctor Sorensen lives? We want the Jerries to think we're out, free, looking for trouble. If they think that they won't search the village and find Curly. Later, we go back for Curly."

There was silence for a while as they slogged through the snow, then Sam asked:

"Did you mean it when you said we'd go back for Curly, Sarge?"

"Course I did. Don't you want to rescue him?" Ted asked sharply.

"Yes." That was all Sam said for the moment, but when they halted a hundred yards farther on at the edge of the railway embankment, he seemed to think he had not said enough, for he went on: "If you'd talked of leaving him, Sarge,

I . . . I think I'd have gone back for him on my own."

"What ? Against orders ?" Ted somehow managed to keep the chuckle out of his voice. Sometimes he thought Sam was too slow for words, while at other times he seemed to be one jump ahead of anyone else.

"I know there'd have been trouble," Sam admitted; "but I'd made up my mind I wasn't going to leave Curly. I'm . . . sort of fond of him."

"And he'd borrow your last penny," China grunted, only to add quickly: "Not that I'd have let you go alone. You couldn't have got Curly out by yourself."

"Well, when you've finished organising a mutiny," Ted suggested quietly, "we'll move. There are a lot of little lights behind us . . . and I think they are probably torches . . . and even in Norway torches don't walk about by themselves."

Sam and China looked back. Spread out along the road they had just left were some forty or more winking lights. It had not taken the Germans long to decide where the Commandos would be. Somewhere between the two road-blocks the Britishers had left the lorry, and the German officer's orders were easy to understand. "Shoot at anything that moves. The Norwegians are not supposed to be out after dark—so if you shoot one of them it won't matter."

Ted ploughed a trail through snow which had not a single footmark in it until their feet broke the crust. Once the Germans found the tracks it would merely be a question of following them until they caught up with their quarry.

For two hours Ted slogged on with a panting Sam, and a grimly silent China at his heels. The going was hard, and they did not know the country. The ground was rising, and growing steeper every minute. Then Ted was halted abruptly by a solid wall of ice-covered rock. Masking his torch until it allowed only a pencil of light to shine, he risked a quick look at the barrier which blocked their way. Though the three Britishers did not know it, this was the foot of the mountain they had crossed to make their attack on the power station.

Directly above them was the snout of the glacier. Even if they had been able to scale the first twenty feet or so of icicle covered rock, they could have got no farther. The glacier snout was smooth and slippery as wet glass.

"Done any rock-climbing, Sam ?" Ted asked, flicking off his light and returning the torch to his breast pocket.

"He's done plenty of rock-eating," China said with a chuckle. "Used to take half-day trips to

Brighton when he was a kid. Always came home sucking a bit of Brighton rock."

"Suppose you think you're funny," Sam said indignantly. "Well, I'll tell you I used to go to Cromer. Now that's a place if you like; a real place. I wouldn't be found dead at Brighton."

"I don't know that *I* want to be found dead in Brighton," Ted interposed, "but if we can't think up something good pretty soon there's a first-rate chance of us being found dead here. We can't go farther, and Jerry is on our heels. Now, get your thinking caps on. I picked you two 'cos of your brains. Like a cig, China? Sam has a few left."

"You'll owe me some smokes before we get back," Sam grunted, beginning to feel for his watertight cigarette tin. "Anyway, Sarge; why are we stopping here? We can turn to left or to right, can't we?"

"Look back, Sam," Ted urged. "The worst of these Jerries is that they're too darned methodical. See the lights? They've got a long line of fellows out. And the two ends of that line are swinging in to this same rock wall. They know we can't go on. They know we can't go back. So they're blocking up the side-runs. The men at the ends of their line will reach this rock barrier long before we can slip out. So, unless we can sprout wings . . . we've had it. Come on, Sam, hand over those cigs. Anybody'd think they were yours."

"They are mine. My cig ration," Sam protested, opening the tin and holding it out to Ted. "It's always the same with you blokes. You kill yourselves smoking your own ration so you can borrow mine."

"We're only doing it for your good, Sammy boy," China chuckled, taking a cigarette, then leaning forward towards Sam's petrol lighter. "You're too young to smoke . . . that's why we take your fags. Come on, give us a light, and keep your glove round it so the Jerries won't see the glow."

They lit up and masking the cigarettes in wet gloved hands squatted on the frozen snow. Behind them the long line of German troops drew slowly nearer. In front of them was the unscalable ice-covered rock face. A minute or so passed, and the only sounds came from the thin wind which moaned eerily from the north, and the occasional creak of leather as first one and then the other of the three men eased into a more comfortable position.

It was left to Sam to break the silence.

"Look, Sarge," he said quietly. "If we hang about here much longer the Jerries will get us for certain. We might drop a few of them, but I'm worried about Curly. If we cop it out here,

Curly's sure to be caught later on. And what about the Norwegian doctor and his wife? We've got to do something for them, haven't we? After all, they took a big risk when they let us in and saved Curly's life."

"I'm thinking, too, Sam," Ted assured him, and dragging his German submachine-gun on to his knees began to feel the mechanism. "Look, while we have a chance we'd better get the feel of these guns. When the balloon goes up we don't want to be held up by a jam. Just get familiar with the gun actions."

"But what about Curly?" Sam persisted, as he began to take off his wet gloves so that he could finger the moving parts of the Schmiesser sub-machine-gun.

"If you have any bright ideas, Sam, out with 'em," Ted ordered. "I'm thinking hard. I don't want the doctor's family to suffer. I don't want Curly to be taken prisoner . . . but we're up against a stone wall. A wall we can't climb. It's shoot it out—and that means no going back home any more—or thinking up some bright idea. If we were angels, Sam, we could fly away," he gave a rueful chuckle as he added: "I don't think China's any angel, and we can't leave him."

"Angels," China snorted. "You'll never have wings, Sarge, if you live to be ten thousand years old. Why, anybody what's been on the barrack square under you will know. . . ."

"I've got an idea," Sam broke in quietly. "What about me drawing them off? I could go down towards them. I've got six of these Jerry magazines. If I kept the Jerries busy for a few minutes you and China might be able to slip away . . . if you kept moving along the foot of this rock wall I'll bet you could do it. The Jerries would be sure to close in on me. What do you think?"

There was a silence for perhaps ten seconds while Ted Harris and China thought over the idea. It would mean Sam's death, but it would give them a slim chance of getting away. Ted finally broke the silence.

"Yes," he breathed the word heavily. "Yes, Sam, that's a first-rate idea."

CHAPTER SIX

TWO-HEADED PENNY

"THAT'S fixed then," Sam said, beginning to rise to his feet. "I've got a wallet here, Sarge. Will you see it goes back to my . . .?"

"Wait a minute, Sam," Ted interrupted. "You're forgetting something. I like your idea. I think it's good; but don't forget I'm the bloke with the three stripes. I'm still the sergeant. When I go back and make my report what are they going to say when I tell 'em I sent Sam down to face . . ."

"They wouldn't ask about me," Sam protested.

"You couldn't do it, anyway," China said firmly. "There's only one bloke can do it, and that's me. Ted . . ."

"Sergeant Harris, please," Ted said cuttingly.

"Sorry, Sarge," China's voice had an amused note in it. "Sorry; but I was just goin' to say as you couldn't do it, either. Cos why ? Cos there's only *you* could organise Curly's rescue. Even if me and Sam did get him away what'd we do then ? The sub's gone back to Blighty by now, and . . ."

"Just tell me something, please, China," Ted Harris said sweetly: "Am I sergeant, or not ?"

126

"There are times when I don't care two hoots whether you are a sergeant or a blinkin' admiral," China assured him, "and this happens to be one of those times. Come off it, Sarge, and act reasonable. You just can't go. You got the brains. I don't want Sam to go. I like him, and I like his sister, she's one of . . ."

"While we're arguing," Sam butted in, "the Jerries are coming nearer." They stared down the dark, snow-covered slope. The long line of winking lights was definitely nearer, swaying and bobbing as the men lurched through the hampering snow. Climbing that long snow slope had been hard work for the three Commandos, and they were in the pink of condition, used to this sort of work, hard as nails from months of slogging over lonely Scottish moors. The Germans were third-rate garrison troops, nothing like as young or as fit as the men they sought. They were coming on quite slowly now, and not very enthusiastically. They knew of that high wall of unclimbable rock, and they knew something about the courage and toughness of the British Commandos. Nevertheless, they were closing the net. The two ends of the line had reached the rock, and were now moving along it.

"Tell you what," China said, diving his hand inside his anorak and feeling for an inside pocket.

"Let's toss for it." He finally produced a coin. "Here you are Ted . . . sorry, *Sarge*. You toss, and I'll call."

"You can't leave me out," Sam said doggedly. "It was my idea."

"Whoever wins this toss will toss with you. How's that sound, Sarge ?"

Ted Harris hesitated.

"I don't like it," he snapped. "I don't like it at all, and if there wasn't a grain of truth in what you say about getting Curly away I wouldn't do it, but . . ."

"Spin the coin and I'll call," China urged. "We're losing time."

The coin was flicked into the air and caught expertly.

"Heads! " China called, and waited while Sam flicked on his masked torch for a second to reveal the penny lying head upwards on Ted's gloved hand.

"Better to be born lucky than rich," China said cheerfully. "Here, Sam, toss."

"You toss and I'll call," Sam suggested.

"Go on, toss," China urged, and pressed the coin into Sam's glove. Sam muttered something and tossed the coin.

"Heads!" China called, and when they looked a second time, there it was again, lying head up on Sam's glove.

"Ta . . . don't pocket that penny," China remonstrated. "It's a lucky one."

"It isn't one of those trick pennies, is it?" Ted asked, suddenly suspicious.

"What?" China gave a snort of disgust and thrust the coin into his pocket as if too hurt to say more. "What happens afterwards, Sarge? Where do we meet afterwards?"

"The railway siding." Ted's voice was gruff to hide his emotion, and he gripped China's right hand in his two. He wrung it for a moment then said: "Don't be taken alive, China. If you are taken prisoner they'll torture you. They'll want to know where we are . . . and you might talk. They use drugs to make people talk. At least, that's what I've been told."

"They won't catch me." China scoffed at the idea. "See you later, then. So long, Sam. By the way, don't forget . . . I owe you three bob. I'll pay you, first time I'm in the money."

Then he was gone, moving away from the rock wall, and heading down towards the slowly moving line of lights.

"We'll head north," Ted Harris decided. "I want to get back to that railway siding if I can. It's from there we'll move when we've got Curly away."

"What do you reckon China's chances are, Sarge?" Sam asked, and there was an unaccustomed huskiness in his voice. "I don't think he ought to have done what he did. Wasn't fair dealings, really."

"What do you mean . . . fair dealings ?" Ted was rubbing the metal of his gun to induce a little warmth in it so that it would not jam through the intense cold.

"Well, that *was* a two-headed penny he used," Sam confessed. "I knew it the moment I looked . . . when you tossed it first time."

"What! Well the . . . Humph. I'll go to sea. Why didn't you tell me ?" Ted demanded angrily.

Sam shrugged.

"It was better that China or I should go, and you know it, Sarge. You've got the brains to get Curly away. If you'd gone out now . . . we'd never have got away."

"Two-headed penny, eh! The twister. . . . I'll have his blood when I get hold of him. Trust that blighter to work a fast one if he got half a chance. All right, Sam, we'll keep close to the rock. When China opens up against the Jerries they'll start closing in . . . that'll be our chance to get through."

They moved slowly, and Ted's face was set in hard lines as he watched the line of lights. The Germans had come up in a half circle, and the two ends had reached the rock barrier. All they had to do, now, was keep closing in and the British Commandos were caught.

Suddenly the quiet of the night was broken. China had opened up with a short burst of fire at the centre of the lights and three of the German lights went out immediately.

Ted halted, and with their backs to the rock wall he and Sam waited and watched. Very quickly all the German torches were switched off, and for a minute or so there was silence. The Germans were waiting for China to start shooting again, when they would immediately plaster the area with a rain of bullets from three sides.

"Hope China doesn't get impatient," Sam murmured.

Ted gave a hard little laugh.

"He won't, Sam," he said confidently. "He's a bit hare-brained at times, and he's impulsive . . . but he's nobody's fool. He knows the minute he starts shooting he'll be the target of a score of guns."

Suddenly the silence was broken by a single shot, the stab of flame seeming to be almost lightning-bright in the thick darkness. It was a chance shot, tempting China to retaliate. Nothing happened. Wherever China was he held his fire.

"They're getting near us, now," Sam whispered; his ears were amazingly sensitive, and he had picked up a guttural whisper which seemed to be less than a dozen yards distant.

Ted laid a warning hand on Sam's mouth, cautioning him not to even whisper now. He, too, had heard a slight crunching, as men moved over the frozen snow, picking their way cautiously.

The two Commandos had settled down against the rocky wall, huddled as close as they could, and trusting to their white camouflage to bring them through safely.

Sam's nerves were taut as fiddle strings. He could hear the Germans now, whispering to one another, and had an idea he could see a vague shadow only a few yards away . . . a shadow which was moving parallel to the rocky wall, and must stumble over them unless a miracle happened.

Ted was on his haunches, every muscle tense. They had one advantage: there was only one person out here on the snow who was not an enemy, so they could shoot almost as they liked. The Germans might easily be shooting one another if they opened up indiscriminately. The disadvantage was that if he and Sam were wounded the game would be up for Curly, and the Norwegian doctor.

The shadows were nearer, now; so near that even Ted could hear the laboured breathing of the Germans. There were three of them blocking

the escape route along the wall. Their guns would
be cocked, and fingers would be taut on triggers.

Bang! It was so unexpected that even Ted
jumped nervously.

The explosion lit up the snow some hundred
yards away, and was made by the last of China's
hand grenades. He had tossed it down the slope,
and the moment the explosion took place, showing a score of figures outlined against the white-
ness, he opened up with a short, accurate burst of
submachine-gun fire.

"Tat-tat-tat-tat-tat-tat-tat-tat."

There were shouts and screams. Then as men
were left blinking owlishly in the darkness which
followed the explosion flash, Germans to the
south opened up with everything they had,
rifles and automatic weapons.

The three Germans near Ted and Sam started
to run, moving away from the rock wall in the
direction of the flashes of China's weapon. They
moved less than a dozen yards before one of them
gave a yell and pitched face down, victim of a
German bullet. The other two flung themselves
down by his side.

The panicky firing went on for about ninety
seconds, during which time bullets flew in all
directions, smashing against the rocky wall,
throwing up little clouds of snow as they skittered
over the frozen surface.

As the last shot echoed across the valley Sam started to his feet. China had given a long wailing yell of:

"Oh . . . Sam . . . Sam . . . oh, I'm hit."

Ted grabbed Sam in a grip which hurt.

"He's bought one," Sam gasped. "We . . ."

Ted was on his feet and dragging Sam northwards.

"But, Sarge . . ." Sam whispered urgently, "We can't . . ."

"Quiet, Sam . . . do you want to die ?"

There was no arguing with Ted at that moment. Sam was no weakling, but Sergeant Harris seemed to possess the strength of two men. He strode away from the scene of the shooting, taking long strides and forcing Sam to do the same.

Behind them a German voice called over the snow, but there was no answer. The German called again, and this time it was an order to the men to move in, and to shoot only if they saw someone trying to get away.

Ted did not speak again until he and Sam had put a hundred yards between them and the trap from which they had just escaped. Then he released his grip and said more gently:

"We couldn't do anything, Sam. China must have been badly hit to yell out like that."

"But if we'd . . ."

"If we'd gone in there, we'd have been dead now," Ted interrupted. "We have two tommy-guns . . . there are probably fifty Germans, maybe a hundred, I don't know. They're nervy. At the first flash of a gun from us they'd riddle us both. Our duty is to get away. We want to get Curly away if we can, and that means stopping the Jerries from searching the village first of all. We'll go down to the railway siding . . . just on the offchance that China managed to get away . . ."

"Get away!" Sam could not hide his astonishment at such a suggestion. "But that yell . . . when he called my name. He must have been badly hurt."

"Maybe he was," Ted conceded, "but I'm not giving up hope. China's as cunning as a bagful of monkeys. He tricked me with a double-headed penny; how do you know that yell wasn't an attempt to trick the Jerries. I hope it was, anyway."

They got down to the siding about ninety minutes later, evaded the guard patrolling the lines of trucks, and hid behind the building where the Diesel engines were housed. It was bitterly cold, and they waited with ears pricked for some sound which would tell them China was alive, and had returned to the agreed rendezvous.

At the end of three hours Ted gave a little

sigh and rose, his limbs stiff with cold and inaction.

"Looks as if he's had it, Sam," he conceded regretfully. "I've cussed him, told him he was a bone-headed nitwit, but he was one of the best. I only hope he died quick. I'd hate to think of the S.S. people getting their hands on him."

"Yes!" That was all Sam could say. His throat was blocked by a big lump. Though he would not put it into words, he had a feeling that their case was pretty hopeless. China dead, Curly wounded and very weak. The submarine which should have taken them back to Scotland would be gone in another twenty-four hours. Those who did not return by her would be written off as either dead, prisoners, or as a last chance, interned in Sweden if they managed the arduous trip across the mountains to that neutral country.

"We've got to move south again, Sam," Ted said, when they had got clear of the siding. "We've got to hit the Jerries again . . . so they'll be sure we are making for the coast. If we can do that I think Curly and Doctor Sorenson are safe."

Their many long-distance training operations had toughened the Commandos until they were able to perform almost incredible feats of endurance. Sam and Ted covered fifteen more miles that night, avoiding a number of road-blocks and villages garrisoned by Germans. The going was hard all the time, for they had to keep off the roads, and the hillsides were covered with snow.

It was about six o'clock in the morning, with no sign yet of daylight, when they stalked a German guard shivering by his sentry box. He had been warned by telephone that British Commandos had escaped a drag-net farther up country, but not even the corporal of the guard had imagined the Commandos could get so far south in such a short time.

Sam came out of the night like a bullet, tackling the sentry from behind and bringing him down with a sudden crash. The snow deadened the sound of his coal-scuttle helmet as it shot across the road.

There was an exclamation from the bigger hut and a tousle-haired N.C.O. ran out to see what was happening. He stopped abruptly when he almost ran into Ted's gun. His hands went above his head at once, while his eyes grew round as saucers.

" *Kommandos!*" he stuttered.

"Right first time," Ted agreed, smiling, then backed the N.C.O. into the hut, in time to cover two more Germans who were hastily pulling on their jackboots.

Sam brought the dazed sentry into the hut.

None of the Germans spoke English, but they understood sign language easily enough, and set about making a hot drink and bringing out food. They were scared. This was the first time they had seen British Commandos, but they had heard plenty about them. They knew what had happened up at the big power station, and were quite willing to take no risks. The N.C.O. did everything without a murmur, even to tying the wrists of his men, and doing the job efficiently. Sam did the same for him, then checked that there were no loose knots.

There was a map on the wall, and while they drank the ersatz coffee and finished off enough food for four men—sausages and black bread, they studied the route to the coast, while the Germans sat in a row on one of the two bunks, silent but watchful.

Ted marked out their route to the head of the fjord, putting a cross at two points where it looked as if they would have to spend the night. Finally they collected every scrap of food there was left, took two cartons of .300 ammunition which would fit their borrowed Schmeisser submachine-guns, then prepared to leave.

Sam ripped out the telephone wires, Ted blew out the oil lamp, and closing the door behind them after building up the little fire in the stove, they walked out into the night.

They stood for a few moments to let their eyes grow accustomed again to the darkness, and it was then that Sam turned to Ted Harris and asked:

"Sarge, what about the map? Have you left it?"

"On the table," Ted agreed. "We don't need it. I've got a map."

"Yes, but you marked a route on it," Sam pointed out, and wondered why Ted chuckled.

"I did . . . and I'm hoping the Jerries will use that map, and the route." Ted was grinning as he spoke. "We want 'em to think we're heading for the coast, Sam boy. We want 'em to watch that route . . . it's a tough route, but it isn't the way we'll go, not now nor later. At the moment we're heading up the valley . . . to see if Curly's any fitter."

Sam rubbed his unshaven chin and smiled wanly. Then shook his head.

"You're too clever for me, Sarge," he admitted. "I'd never have thought of that. I'm afraid I can only think of one thing at a time."

"Don't worry about that, Sam. I've noticed that when you do think . . . it usually means getting us out of a hole." Ted patted Sam on the shoulder, then said: "We'll walk up the road a stretch, and leave it at some point where our footprints won't show. We've got to hide-up, now, for a day or two . . . and it isn't going to be easy."

Three days later, at the close of a short, wintry day, the two Britishers walked back into the village where Doctor Sorensen and his family lived. They had come to see if Curly Bates was fit to travel.

Ted and Sam looked tougher than ever, now. It was four days since they had enjoyed the luxury of a wash, and seven days since either of them had shaved. They were leaner in the face, for there had been little food during the past days, and lying out in a hole they had dug in the snow on the hillside did not kill their appetite.

During those three days they had worked out the time-table of the trains which ran on the narrow gauge railway, and Ted had booked them down. They might need a third-class ticket to the coast, if Curly was able to travel. They had discussed the fate of China Brown, and decided he would have to be reported " Missing . . . presumed dead." China would not stop fighting until his last bullet had gone, and there had been plenty of Germans to shoot at, and to shoot at him.

One great thrill had come their way during the long and weary wait. A British Mosquito had flown over the valley, apparently taking aerial shots of the wrecked power station. German fighter planes had been summoned and it did both Britishers good to see the reconnaisance plane dive down towards the snow-covered valley at a speed which left miniature vapour trails smoking from its wing tips. The German fighters had not had a chance to fire a single burst.

The village was its dark, silent self when Ted and Sam walked into the main street. Since the raid on the power station the Germans had put a strict curfew on everyone, with the threat that any Norwegian seen in the streets after dark would be shot at once.

Ted walked boldly up to the doctor's front door and gave the V-sign, three sharp taps on the woodwork, followed by an unmistakable scrape with the muzzle of his gun.

Within a minute the door was opened, and closed quickly again when the two Commandos were inside. The doctor's wife brought a small oil lamp, and it was obvious she was frightened, Ted began to apologise, but the doctor waved a hand for silence, and ushered his visitors to the top of the cellar steps, indicating that they should go down.

For a moment Ted Harris hesitated, then nodded and felt his way down the stone steps, Sam at his heels. They both stopped, however, a moment later when they heard a key grate in the lock.

The doctor had locked them in the cellar!

CHAPTER SEVEN

FIRST STEPS FOR HOME

SAM half turned, but Ted grabbed him by the coat sleeve drawing him down into the dark, bitterly cold cellar.

"Is he going to give us away?" Sam asked. "Why has he locked us in?"

"He wouldn't turn traitor," Ted whispered. "Something must have gone wrong. Perhaps the Jerries found Curly."

"Oh, lor," Sam groaned at the thought. "Poor old Curly."

"Shut up, you groaning pessimist," Ted hissed. "I only said they ' might ' have found him. In any case we . . . sssssh!" He stopped, for even down in the cellar they had heard the insistent "rat-tat-tat-tat-tat" on the front door of the house.

In the silence which followed they heard the quick patter of feet on the boards of the narrow hall.

"The doctor's wife," Ted murmured. "Quick, lightish steps, Sam. Too quick and too light for a man."

A moment or so later they heard voices, loud

guttural voices, followed by the sound of boots being kicked against the snow scraper. Germans . . . and coming into the house. Sam quietly pushed his safety catch to the "off" position, moved a foot to one side, and waited. If Germans did start to come down to the cellar they would soon be struck off the pay-roll.

The voices faded as the visitors were led through to the dining-room at the back of the house. Ted and Sam stood and waited. They dared not move about for fear their movements were heard. They grew colder and colder, and by the luminous dial of Ted's watch two hours crept by before anything happened. Then there was a faint squeaking sound from the end of the cellar.

Ted whipped out his torch, and a moment later the white beam was shining full into the face of a small boy, whose eyes looked unnaturally big in the brilliant light.

"I am Erik," he whispered, and came forward soundlessly.

"How have you got in here?" Ted asked, staring in amazement at the boy who appeared to be about eleven years old. He was clad in pyjamas which were of one piece, almost like a footballer's training suit. They were dirty and damp in places.

"I come through wood chute," the boy whispered, and from within his pyjamas he brought a loaf of bread and a chunk of cheese. "My mother is sorry she cannot send better food."

"Better food!" Sam gulped, reaching out for the bread. "Anything is better than the ache I've got behind my belt."

He carved the loaf into two halves and did the same for the cheese, while Ted questioned the boy.

"Could we get out the same way, Erik ?"

"No, sir. I am small . . . and I can only just get down."

"Who are the visitors upstairs ?" Ted went on, taking a bite of bread and a piece of cheese.

"German soldiers," Erik replied. "Please, I must tell you what father says, then I go back . . . or perhaps I shall be caught."

"Go ahead, Erik," and Ted switched off his light so as not to waste the battery.

"Mother did not expect you to-night. There has been much trouble in the past three days," Erik said quickly. "We learn of the things you do. The fight on the hillside, when there were many Germans wounded. Then the oil tanks which were set on fire. We are all very glad. The Germans are now frightened . . . for they are saying there must be a lot of commando soldiers here, since you have attacked five times."

"Cor, stone a crow," Ted murmured, his voice charged with amazement. "Sam, they didn't kill China after all. We . . . sorry, son, go on I'm interrupting."

"Because of these attacks the Germans have now put soldiers to live in every house in the village . . . they think we hide some Commando soldiers. We have four Germans, and . . ."

"What about the two men left here?" Ted interrupted. "The wounded soldier and the Norwegian, Nels Larssen? Have they been caught?"

"Father got them away," Erik said proudly, and added: "We would not let anyone be caught, sir. We hate the Germans."

"Thank goodness for that," Sam mumbled, stuffing more bread and cheese into his mouth. "Where are they now?"

"Father put them where the Germans would never suspect," Erik said, and there was a mischievous chuckle in his voice as he went on: "They hide in the rafters of a shed in the railway siding. German soldiers use it every day."

"Boy, oh boy," Ted muttered in admiration. "Tell your dad, and your mother, that I think they're marvellous. What do you say, Sam?"

"Ah-whum-grum-phup." That was Sam's way of agreeing when he had a mouth crammed with dry bread and strong cheese.

"Sam agrees with me," Ted chuckled. "And if . . ."

"Sir," Erik interrupted. "You are to leave here not later than eleven o'clock, and you are to go by the attic window. Nels Larssen will come to-night for food, and news of you. He does not know that about midnight last night one of the Germans went out on to the roof . . . and stayed there throughout the night. If Nels comes, he will be caught. He plans to come at one o'clock to see . . ."

"Okay," Ted interrupted. "We'll get out as soon as possible. Can we use the front door?"

"No, sir. The Germans lock it when they come in, and they keep the key until they leave in the morning. You will have to go out by the attic window. And . . . please, be very careful. If you are heard, and caught, then my father will be shot. The Germans are very angry."

"Leave it to us, son," Ted patted the boy on the shoulder. "Thanks an awful lot. What time would be best . . . ten o'clock, eleven?"

"Father said eleven. The Germans usually play cards until nearly twelve. Now I must go. Mother will unlock the cellar door when she goes to bed at ten minutes to eleven. Good luck . . . I wish I could fight for Norway."

"You're not doing so bad, son," Ted told him. "Helping us means you are smacking Hitler in the eye. When the war's over . . . I'll come and visit you, and then I'll be able to thank your mum and dad. Cheerio . . . and keep your chin up. One day the Jerries will be on the run . . . and they won't run fast enough."

"Cheerio, sir . . . and I wish you good fortune."

Ted flicked on his light to help the boy across the wood littered floor of the cellar. They watched him squeeze his way up the narrow wood-chute. How he would get back into the house they did not know.

When he had vanished and the last little scraping sound had faded, Ted gave a sigh.

"They've got guts, these folks, Sam . . . loads of guts, even the kids, eh? The Jerries can't beat folk like that."

"Just about on a par with China Brown, Sarge," Sam whispered. "It must have been him . . . kicking up a rumpus. Fancy firing oil tanks."

"Hm!" That was all the comment Ted had to make. He squatted on his haunches, his back against the cold stone of the wall, and munched his dry bread and cheese. He was trying to decide what they must do. China Brown on the rampage did not make things easier, for the Germans would be on their toes. Probably have double guards on everything.

"Think we'll meet up with China again?" Sam asked, breaking a long silence.

"He's probably sailed for home, now," Ted grunted. "China has the luck of Old Nick, and he wouldn't waste time getting away. Pinched a boat. . . ."

"What's the matter?" Sam asked, as Ted stopped abruptly.

"Pinched a boat . . . yes," Ted whispered. Then in a fierce whisper went on: "That's what we'll have to do, Sammy boy. Get down to the fjord and grab a boat. I don't fancy trying to cross the mountains into Sweden, and I'm durned certain I'm not stopping here. We'll do that, Sam . . . ever done any sailing?"

"I'm all right if I've got sea-sickness pills," Sam pointed out. "If I don't have them . . . it's just horrible."

At five minutes to eleven they heard the key turn very quietly in the cellar door lock. They waited a few minutes to allow Mrs. Sorensen to get upstairs to her room, then they crept up to the ground floor. They could hear a murmur of voices from the dining-room. The four Germans were either chatting or passing the time away playing cards.

Up the creaky stairs, then up on to the snow-covered roof. The stairs were shining from an almost cloudless sky, and it seemed almost light up there.

"Makes you feel as if you was undressed, don't it, Sarge?" Sam whispered, quietly closing the attic skylight, then sifting snow into the cracks so that no one could possibly suspect the skylight had been opened.

When they got down to street level it was like walking through a dead world. The villagers were all indoors; the Germans were indoors. Even the sentry guarding the entrance to the Corps Headquarters was huddled in the doorway in an effort to get out of the bitter cold.

Forty minutes later Ted and Sam were in the siding, having scaled the wire fence as far from the road as possible. They tried three of the sheds before there was a reply to Ted's whispered:

"Curly . . . Curly Bates, Sergeant Harris here."

Five minutes later they were reunited. It took so long for Curly to get down, for he was hampered with his wounded arm, now strongly encased in plaster. The Yorkshireman wanted all the news, but Ted would allow no gossip.

"Tell you everything later, Curly," he said. "I want to get out of here as quick as poss. Now listen carefully. We're going down to the coast. Nels, am I right in thinking the railway line is all downhill?"

"Practically all the way," the Norwegian agreed.

"Would a truck free-wheel?"

Nels thought for a moment, then nodded.

"I think it would, once it was pushed out of the sidings. Here, of course, it is level."

"Good. This is what we do," Ted began. "I'm going out to start a bit of trouble. As soon as I've drawn the guards from the siding . . . you push a truck on to the line. Get it rolling, and stop it about half a mile down the track. Got it?

"What about you?" Sam asked anxiously. "Wouldn't it be better if I drew the guards away, and . . ."

"No it wouldn't," Ted cut in. "And will you try and remember, Sam Foster—*Private* Sam Foster, that I am the sergeant. I've got the three stripes. Don't be so anxious to be a hero, Sam. I'm paid for being the boss . . . and in this commando game the boss decides who takes the risks. Now . . . synchronise your watches with mine".

They compared watches, set them exactly right with Ted's, it was just a minute past mid-night.

"In ten minutes I'll start firing. Give the guards about five minutes to gather round the entrance . . . then get busy with the truck. If I don't join you inside half an hour . . . you'll know I've bought it. Curly will be in charge. Any questions?"

"Just one, Sarge," Curly said, and the darkness hid the twinkle in his eyes. "Can I have your footer boots if you don't get back? The black ones in your locker back at the barracks?"

"What!" Ted exploded, then spat out in disgust. "Hear that, Sam? That's a pal, for you. Hoping

I won't get back so he can swipe my best football boots. Curly . . . you'll never wear those boots. I'll be with you inside half an hour. See you later!" He went, moving across the snow like a shadow.

Prompt to the dot of the ten-minute time-limit there was a sudden sharp crackle of automatic fire from the distant roadway. It was answered within seconds by a single rifle-shot. There was another short burst of fire, and more rifle shots. In the silence which followed the sound of shouts could be heard. The German guards patrolling the siding were hastening to the gates to reinforce their comrades there.

Sam, Curly and Nels Larssen moved out along the track. They found an empty truck as near the main line as possible, uncoupled it, took off the brakes, then began to push.

It seemed as if the truck would never move, but once it started to roll the rest was easy. Soon they were trotting, and when the end of the siding was reached Sam had to race as fast as he could to catch the truck and apply the brakes.

All the time they had been pushing at the truck there had been spasmodic bursts of firing. Now, however, as Sam clambered into the truck, then leaned over the side to give Curly a hand up, the firing increased. It sounded like a pitched battle.

Nels took off the brakes, and trotted alongside

the truck as it slowly began to move along the gentle gradient. He kept applying the brakes to prevent the speed increasing too much, and when he judged they were half a mile from the sidings, he swung hard on the brake handle, bringing the truck to a squealing stop.

In the quiet they listened to the sharp crackle of rifle and automatic fire from the direction of the siding.

"I didn't know Ted had so many magazines with him," Sam pondered. "In fact I'm sure he hadn't."

"I wouldn't be too sure," Curly grunted. "Sounds like a pitched battle to me. He'll be lucky if he gets back. Keep your eye on the ticker, Sam. He said half an hour, and then to up-stakes and scram."

Slowly the minute finger of Sam's wrist watch moved round, shining faintly luminous in the darkness.

"How long has he got ?" Curly finally asked.

"Five minutes," Sam lied. They had already been there thirty-five minutes.

"We'll give him another ten," Curly decided, and then sniffed. "You're a poor liar, Sam. I know he's already had his half hour. I can see the watch from here."

"Well, you wouldn't want to leave him, would you ? Ted wouldn't leave you."

"Who's talking about leaving him?" Curly growled. "It's Ted's orders . . ."

"Whose orders ?" The voice came from the darkness a few yards away. "Who've you got with you . . . apart from Privates Foster and Bates, and Larssen."

"Ted!" Sam and Curly yelped the name together.

Ted Harris ordered Larssen to climb into the truck, then the took off the brakes, leaned his shoulder against the buffers, and within seconds the thing was on the move again. Ted scrambled up, helped by willing hands. He laid his gun down, wiped his face, then said:

"Now, listen, you two. In Civvy Street my name is Ted Harris; but while I'm in the bloomin' army I'm *Sergeant* Ted Harris to folks like you. I—stand upright when I'm talking to you, Curly. Get your hands out of your pockets!"

Nels Larssen stared in amazement at the dimly seen figure of Sergeant Harris. He just could not understand these British; but then he could not see the twinkle in the eyes of Ted Harris, nor see the grins on the faces of Curly and Sam. They understood Ted, and knew he was merely enjoying himself. When he talked like that he had usually done something that had pleased him a lot.

"What's been happening, Sarge ?" Sam asked, leaning against the truck side as the rapidly increasing speed began to shake them all from side to side. "It sounds as if somebody's been wasting a lot of ammo."

"They're still wasting it," Ted chuckled. "They're keeping themselves warm . . . fighting an army of British Commandos. Oh, lor, Sam . . . gimme a cig before I die laughing."

Not until they were all smoking Sam's precious cigarette ration did Ted begin to explain.

"There's a road block about half a mile or so from the railway siding. I reckoned any firing would bring the guards along . . . but I certainly didn't expect them to come quite as fast as they did. Those guards from the road-block must have run like hares."

He drew deep on his cigarette, so that the end glowed brightly enough to light up his lean, dirty, and unshaven face.

"I fired a short burst at the gate guards," he went on, "and then the row started. I kept firing an odd shot from different places, just to kid them there were a few of us, and then a gang arrived from the road block. They were in a real, tearing hurry. I fired a burst at 'em, then scooted, and left them to it. They started firing back, and of course their shots were going round the siding gates, so everybody was happy. They'd got their own little war. No need for me to interfere at all," and he chuckled.

Little was said during the next hour, for the truck was hurtling along down the gradient, over rails slippery with ice, and at times it seemed as if they would all be flung into eternity.

Luckily there were short stretches here and there where the track was level, and the speed decreased a little. The last four kilometres to the fjord head was the worst, for the gradient grew very steep, and in a desperate attempt to prevent them rushing straight down into the fjord, or crashing into waggons in a siding, Ted climbed over the side of the truck, and got his foot on to the brake lever. Sam and Nels held him, but it was a breath-taking minute or so, and even Ted was silent when they hauled him back.

The truck wheels threw off sparks, sometimes locked for a short period, and then they bumped and skidded along the rails.

"Hope everybody can swim," Curly cried, breaking a long, tense silence among them. "I've got a feeling we'll stop when we shoot off into the water."

The truck stopped, however, about four hundred yards from the waterfront, and when Curly had been helped down they all squatted by the truck side and got back their breath.

"I've pinched some rides in my time," Curly finally murmured, "but in future I'll pay for 'em all. That's the worst, and the last, ride I ever take free. Sarge, I'll bet my hair's silvery now."

"Which one do you mean?" Ted chuckled. "The one that grows above your right ear, or the one you curl in the middle of your bald nut?"

"Funny man, eh?" Curly snorted. "Let me tell you, Sarge, I pay as much for my haircuts as you do."

"It isn't for cutting the hair," Ted pointed out, "It's what they call a search fee. He cuts it for nothing, and just makes you pay for the time he spends looking for it. Anyway . . . we'd better be moving."

They came to a small siding. It was protected by a seven-foot wire-fence and on the other side they could see a German sentry, marching along the quay, occasionally swing his arms to keep himself warm.

Sam went over the wire to see what boats were moored at the quay, and came back twenty minutes later with a report that there were four big armed launches, something like the British Air-Sea-Rescue boats, two or three small fishing-boats, and a freighter of about a thousand tons.

"Move we take one of the launches," Curly said. "They're fast, and if they're armed we're all right if a Jerry fighter spots us before we get home."

"That's a good idea," Sam agreed.

"It's a rotten idea," Ted said decisively.

"Anything I suggest is rotten," Curly snapped. "What's wrong with it ?"

"Know anything about big marine Diesel engines ?" Ted asked gently. "You've probably got three engines, each about six or seven hundred horse power. I can drive a car, I drove the Diesel train—but high-powered marine engines are a different matter. And there's another thing." He paused.

"Go on, I'll bite." Curly muttered. "At least I did suggest something."

"Who's going to navigate ?" Ted asked. "We might start the thing, we might get up speed . . . and then pile ourselves on the beach somewhere. I wouldn't like that."

"Perhaps Nels could help," Curly suggested, but the Norwegian shook his head. He was an electrical engineer, and knew little or nothing about marine engines.

"Perhaps some of the crew sleep aboard," Sam suggested. "If they did . . . we'd be all right, wouldn't we ?"

Ted slowly shook his head.

"I can't see 'em sleeping aboard when there's comfortable billets so close to the waterfront. They might leave a watchman aboard, but . . ." He stopped and began to stroke his stubble-covered chin. The other three watched him and waited. Sam and Curly knew the signs. Ted had an idea. Finally he nodded.

"Yes," he said, half to himself. "It might work." and left them waiting for another full minute before adding: "Listen, we might get a crew . . . but it means putting our eggs all in one basket if you see what I mean. It'll be win or bust. Blighty or a blanket . . . home or a funeral for the four of us. Are you game ?"

Sam and Curly nodded immediately. Nels agreed when he understood that the chance they proposed to take could mean freedom . . . or death.

Ted explained his scheme, and when he was sure that even Nels understood everything, they climbed the wire as soon as the German sentry was at the far end of his beat. As the men turned to march back towards the wire four figures huddled together, Nels in the middle so that his dark clothes would not show against the white of the snow.

The German strode briskly along, grounded his rifle, then Ted moved.

CHAPTER EIGHT

WIN OR BUST!

LIKE a leopard for silence and ferocity, Ted swept through the air, one hand reaching for the German's mouth, the other arm encircling the man's chest. The sentry probably never knew what happened, for he was out before he hit the snow. Ted threw his rifle over the wire, fastened his arms behind him with his own belt, then left him there. Donning the coal-scuttle helmet he began to march along the quay, his "beat" clearly outlined in the snow, a narrow track worn by every sentry who had patrolled that quay since the first snow fell.

The second sentry was marching from the other end of the quay. Ted walked more slowly, so that the German reached the end of his beat, in the middle of the quay, a moment or so before he got there.

There was a little noise when Ted dealt with this sentry, for the man's helmet came off and made a slight metallic "clank" as it fell. Ted had had to strike the man with his fist, and his knuckles were bleeding when he dragged the limp sentry to one side.

He stood staring towards the guard hut, but no
sound came from it. The relief were still happy
inside there, whether sleeping or sitting around a
stove Ted did not know.

Moving along nearer the hut he waited, gun
at the ready, but the night remained silent.
Minutes passed, while ghostly figures moved
from one German sea-going launch to another.
Finally Curly came to report.

"There were watchmen aboard the boats,
Sarge. We've got 'em all. Want 'em out here ?"

"Got any explosives ?"

"Yes, Nels made one of the Jerries talk. We've
got a box of grenades."

"Okay, you know what to do; get cracking."

Curly spun on his heels and went back to the
nearest vessel. A minute passed, and then from
the guard hut came the sharp " brrrrrr-rrrr-rrrrr-
rrrr" of a telephone bell.

As if it had been a signal there was a sudden,
muffled explosion from one of the big launches.
There was a second almost immediately, and as
Ted turned to look in that direction flames lit
up the scene, and wreckage belched into the air.
The ruddy glow vanished at once, but a moment
or so later a lesser glow began to shine from a
tangle of woodwork which had been a deck-
house. Flames licked upwards.

Ted did not look round as other explosions

added their noise to the night. The snow-covered quay was now shining pink in the glow of explosions and flames from the first big launch.

A German rushed out of the guard hut, hurriedly clapping his coal-scuttle helmet on. Ted fired a short burst, and the soldier turned back, bumping into a second man. From the side window of the guard hut a gun spat flame, and Ted hunched his shoulders a little as something which might have been a homing bee droned past his right ear.

Tac-a-tac-taca-taca-taca! The vicious hammering of his submachine-gun added more noise to the crackle of burning wood and the clatter and splash of debris falling into the water. There was a yell of pain from the hut, and Ted moved quickly nearer the waterfront.

From the other side of the fjord came the echoes of his shots, while from the wooden houses on the other side of the three rows of railway trucks came shouts.

Ted turned to look to his right. He had a glimpse for a moment of Sam herding five men through the wire, and sending them hurrying on their way with a shot at their heels. Then he dropped flat as bullets whistled about him from the direction of the guard hut. The men in there had got over the first panic.

A quick burst of fire aimed at the side window of the hut stopped the firing. He followed it a few seconds later with another burst, then scrambled to his feet and leapt aboard the one motor launch which had not been damaged by bomb explosions. Sam Foster followed him aboard a few seconds later. Curly Bates was already there, and Nels Larssen.

Curly was squatting out of danger with four German-type hand grenades at his feet.

"They don't work exactly like ours, Sarge," he said, and with a grin added: "But they don't seem a bad bomb just the same. You do this . . . and then there's the 'whoof.' They're not bad eggs at all."

"Take one each," Ted said curtly. "Then get to your posts. I'll stay on deck. And remember . . . if things go right you've each to stick to your posts for a long time. Pity China wasn't here. We could have used him."

Sam led the way below. Ted remained on deck, hidden from anyone on the quay by the deck housing. The next few minutes would be tricky. There were burning launches fore and aft of the one which held the British soldiers. Everything depended on whether the Germans came aboard this particular one and tried to get it away before it, too, caught fire.

"If they are suspicious, and think we're aboard this," Ted muttered, "then we've had our chips."

He tensed a moment later, for men were arriving

at the far gate, and yells to the guard hut brought one man out at a darting run to open the gate. An officer ran in with a crowd of men at his heels. The officer was shouting angrily, and wanting to know what had happened.

Before the unhappy corporal of the guard could even begin to speak there was a sudden crackle of fire from the farther end of the quay; an automatic weapon spat a continuous stabbing fire, and three or four men dropped in the snow. A moment later there was not a German standing. The uninjured were down and pouring a hail of lead towards the other gate. By this time the firing had stopped.

Ted waited, tense, expectant. The crackle of rifle fire died away at a command from the officer. Soldiers ran out through the gate to take the unseen attacker in the rear. Meanwhile the crackling of burning wood grew louder, and was reinforced a few moments later by a loud "whoosh" from the first boat to have bombs explode in her. A great curling mushroom of fire shot into the sky, fringed by black smoke, and debris scattered about.

"Oil tanks gone up," Ted murmured. "Hope it doesn't scare them from trying to save our boat."

For a moment or so it looked as if no attempt would be made to get to safety the one big launch which was not in flames. The Army officer was yelling orders, but no one moved. Then, on to the quay ran a man in the uniform of the German Navy. Behind him were four others in naval uniform. They stopped for a moment, then at a single word of command from the naval officer, the four ratings followed him at the double.

By now the night had been turned almost into day. Three big launches were flaming furiously, and the first one whose oil tanks had exploded was beginning to settle in the water. The light breeze blowing was sending great tongues of flame sweeping across the bows of the vessel still unharmed.

Ted shrank back as far as he could as the German naval men leapt aboard. One man clattered down to the engine-room, the officer ran to the little wheel-house, the other two cast off the mooring lines, then yelled that all was clear.

For perhaps thirty seconds nothing happened. Then there was a slight vibration from below. The powerful marine Diesels were turning over, the high pressure air starters breaking the oil seals which were tending to glue the pistons inside the cylinders.

Ted was holding his breath, praying that the Diesels would wake to life. If they did, if these four German naval men could get this craft away from the quay, then there was a sporting chance of freedom. Four Germans, and against them three British Commandos and a Norwegian who hated anything and everything German.

A sound from behind Ted made him turn quickly, and he whipped up his tommy-gun at the sight of a dripping figure hauling itself out of the water. His gun swung for a blow, for he did not want to risk a shot, but before the butt could crash home the figure spoke:

"Blimey, Sarge . . . hold it."

It was not often that Sergeant Ted Harris could be taken completely off balance, but he was certainly taken aback now, for the voice he heard was one he had never thought to hear again . . . the voice of China Brown.

Bending down he gave China a hand, holding him steady as he stood, gasping, and with icy water running off him in streams.

"Talk about . . . a cold . . . shower," China gasped, wiping water from his face. "Didn't reckon it'd be as cold as that."

"Don't worry," Ted said crisply, "you'll soon be warm. Look at those flames. If we don't get out of here quick this boat will be on fire."

As he finished speaking there was a sudden low rumble from below decks, and the big launch began to tremble as the first of the mighty Diesels woke to life.

"Could have joined you sooner," China

grunted, "if I'd been sure—it was you. Saw you creep—along; but I've been—hiding down here for what seems like two or three days. Thought you—might be Jerries—on the prowl for me! You took a long time—to get—here, didn't you?"

"Had to go back for Curly," Ted grunted, cocking an eye on the quayside to see if they were moving, and then looking for'ard to where the two German seamen were working like fiends, drawing buckets of water and sluicing them along the decks in an effort to keep the long, searing flames from the launch ahead from setting the planking ablaze.

"I'm reporting losin' my tommy-gun," China whispered, drawing closer to his sergeant. "I'm telling you now . . . then you'll know it was in action. I started the shootin' on the quay— then I'd to dive in the drink to get away from 'em."

For a moment Ted Harris forgot the flame-lit quay, and the trembling underfoot. China's last shots at the Germans had certainly been a big help, for it had made the soldiers rushing on to the quay turn their attention away from the one big launch not in flames. If they had decided to board that particular launch then Ted, Sam, Curly and Nels would have been either captured at once, or of they had resisted must certainly

have been killed in the gun battle which would
have followed.

He wanted to ask China how he had managed to
get away with a whole skin from the snow-
covered hillside where they had been trapped by
the Germans. He and Sam had got away because
China had acted as "decoy duck," drawing the
German fire so that his two comrades could get
away. There was no chance to ask further
questions, however, for there was a sudden boil of
foam at the stern of the launch. The officer in
the wheel-house could not afford to waste a
moment, and he had rung down to the engine-
room for every ounce of speed the man below
could give him.

Using full rudder and only one engine the man
at the wheel began to edge the launch away from
the quayside—taking her from her position as
sandwich between two fiercely burning vessels.
It was going to be touch and go, for the first
vessel to go up in flames was now awash, and
like a great roaring torch. Her fuel tanks had
exploded, and the oil was surging out on to the
water, flashing to fire the moment it met the air,
and setting the water bubbling and hissing.

The thrumming of the deck under Ted's feet
increased, telling of a second Diesel beginning to
work. On the quay the German soldiers who had
been hurriedly running out lengths of fire-hose

had now been ordered back. The heat was so great that the lengths of hose were beginning to smoke and what was more there was no water to fight the fires with. The intense cold had frozen the supply back in the pipes.

Slowly but surely the launch worked her bows away from the quay, while great tongues of flame from the sinking vessel ahead swept over her so that her paintwork lifted in great blisters which popped into flame, and then began to run down the wood and metal-work. The two sailors, alternately sluicing buckets of water over themselves and then over the smoking paintwork and timbering, were being encouraged, and bullied, into sticking to their task by the officer in the wheel-house. He was partially protected by the thick plate-glass, though one or two panes had cracked under the intense heat.

Swinging round in a quarter circle the launch moved away from the danger, and when she was about a hundred yards from the quay the engines were cut to quarter speed.

Ted thrust his tommy-gun into the hands of China and said crisply:

"Come on, China, we've got to keep this old schooner on the move. I'm going to take charge of the wheel-house. There are a couple of sailors up there . . . at the sharp end. You take 'em below. There's only one more German down there: the engineer. Hand these two sailors over to Sam and Curly. Send Nels up to me, then you can get a change of clothes."

"Is there some below ?" China asked, taking the gun and cocking it.

"There'll be at least two German sailors down there who are probably feeling pretty hot at the moment," Ted said, grinning. "I dare say they might like to feel the coolness of wet clothing . . . anyway, you can suggest it to 'em."

"S-s-s-sure I will," China chattered, trying to still the rattling of his teeth. "Share and share alike always was my motto. I've had the cold and they've had the hot stuff. Now we can change about. Okay, Sarge, I'm ready."

They strode quickly along the deck until they were abreast of the wheel-house. The officer was leaning out of the other door, shouting angrily to the two sailors who were trying to put out half a dozen very small fires where molten paint had gathered and was burning.

Ted climbed into the wheel-house, and the German naval man must have felt the slight vibrations caused by Ted's thirteen stones. He half turned, his mouth open to make some remark. The words, whatever they were, never left his lips. He saw a grim, white-clad figure holding a hand grenade, and behind Ted the sodden figure of China Brown, equally grim looking, and perhaps more frightening because of the sub-machine-gun he clutched.

"*Mein Gott!*" The German gasped, his voice a half-strangled whisper.

"Same to you," Ted murmured, grinning. "Come in and be introduced."

The German answered the persuasive wave of the hand grenade and turned into the wheel-house. Ted indicated the dials and levers beside the small wheel, then waved a hand out towards the night. "Get moving, brother. We're in a hurry."

The German gulped, looked out at the two seamen still drawing buckets of water from over the starboard side of the launch, still working furiously to put out the one or two small spots of burning paint still showing, then he looked out through the side window at the flaming torches of the others of the fleet of sea-going motor launches. He understood, now, why this disaster had come out of the night. Commandos! The word was an explanation for many things.

He looked again at the unshaven, dirty, lean face of the British sergeant, then he nodded. He moved two small metal levers. Two lights came in on a small dashboard. They were red, but after a moment or so first one, then the other

changed to green, and with each change there
came a difference in the vibrations underfoot.

"That's a good boy," Ted nodded approval as
he felt the long, powerful launch begin to move
more quickly away from the scene of the fires.
Then to China: "In a minute, when the blokes
ashore won't be able to decide what's happening
out here . . . take those two lads down below.
I'm sure they must be hot and tired. Don't
forget to send Nels Larssen up here . . . I may
want him as an interpreter."

"Okay, Sarge." China squeezed water from his
sodden right sleeve, then asked: "Got a cig,
Sarge?"

"Sam's the ration carrier," Ted told him. "He
may have a smoke left. Tell him to send one up
for me, if he has. I could do with a smoke."

"You would . . . like a cigarette?" It was
the German, his right hand going to his coat
pocket.

"Don't bother, I'll get 'em myself." As he
spoke Ted moved across like lightning, clamping
the German's hand in his pocket. When he
allowed the man to take it out he was clutching
a neat, Italian-made automatic pistol. "When
you ' smoke ' one of these somebody is likely to
get hurt, pal. Don't try games like that, they don't
work with us."

The German shrugged.

"Do you blame me?" and his English was almost perfect. "This iss my ship. I am *Kapitan* Spengler, and got this command only three weeks ago."

"Too bad, Captain," Ted commiserated. "It's what they call the fortunes of war. Now it's *my* ship. Anyway, you take orders from me. Steer for the sea, Captain."

Spengler's eyes narrowed a little and he shook his head.

"That iss impossible, Sergeant. No one can get to the sea by night. Not without lights . . . and lights are forbidden. Better wait for dawn." It will be here soon . . . the sky begins to lighten a little even now."

"We're waiting for nothing," Ted growled, "and if . . . oh, hallo, Sam. I was just going to . . ."

"China," Sam yelped, and gave the dripping China Brown a terrific hug. "How'd you get here? We thought you were dead. How'd you get away from the Jerries on the hillside?"

"First question . . . how'd I get here," China said, grinning broadly. "I have been waiting for you coming for ages. Saw you come . . . but couldn't be sure whether it was you or not. When I heard the explosions . . . knew it must be Ted and the boys . . ."

"Sergeant Harris," Ted said, clicking his heels, but grinning.

"Sorry . . . *Sergeant* Harris," China agreed. "I fired a burst at the reinforcements, and when they sent somebody round the back of the trucks to cut me off I dropped into the drink and swam here. As for getting away from the Jerries on the hillside . . . I just got 'em firing at one another . . . from each side, and while the mob in the middle were busy ducking . . . yours truly walked through the lines. I'd one or two near squeaks . . . a graze on the neck, and a parting in my hair."

"You might have been killed," Sam gasped, horrified.

"If I'd stopped there, Sam boy, I would have been killed," China chuckled. "Anyway, a miss is as good as a mile, so . . ."

"We'll celebrate on Saturday," Sam glowed with enthusiasm. "It's my birthday, and I know there'll be a whacking big cake waiting . . ."

"Yes, and it'll wait a long time if you stand there nattering," Ted broke in. "China . . . take those two Jerry sailors below. Sam . . . you'd better see if there's any machine-guns mounted above the wheel-house. I thought I saw twin guns. Get 'em ready. We may need them."

"Okay, Sarge." Sam left the wheel-house and

climbed to a gun post slightly behind, and a little higher than the wheel-house while China Brown took two horrified German seamen down to the engine-room, menacing them with Ted's gun.

"Now, as I was saying," Ted turned to Captain Spengler. "We'll head for the open sea, at speed. Whoop her up, *Kapitan*."

"It iss suicide," the German snarled, "and I vill not . . ."

"Say that again," Ted urged.

"You are quite mad," Spengler snapped, but he moved two little levers. Two red lights came in on a dashboard. After a moment one changed to green and at once there was an increased vibration from underfoot. The trembling increased as the second light winked out and a green one came in. Two of the Diesels were now running at wide-open throttle, their propellers churning up a tremendous wash of foam, as the big launch slowly built up speed.

"Ve must have a light," Spengler said. "The fjord narrows."

"Okay, switch on," Ted snapped, "and don't forget . . . if there's any shooting you'll be right in the thick of it."

Behind them the waters were ruddy from the flames leaping high from the doomed launches. Ahead of them the dark waters were now lit by a single broad path of white from the searchlight on top of the cabin. A great wall of water reared up on each side of the launch as the speed crept up from fifteen to twenty knots, then to twenty-five knots.

Sam called down to Ted:

"Sarge, somebody's trying to contact us from the right there . . . see the light winking in and out ? It's morse . . . but I can't make out what they're saying."

"You should have learned German when you were a kid," Ted yelled back, "then you might have known. Here . . . this looks like a signalling lamp. Answer them. It's only polite to give 'em an answer."

There was no comment from Sam as he took the signalling lamp handed up to him from the wheel-house window. Sam had come to the Commandos from the Royal Corps of Signals. He mastered the working of the signalling lamp, then asked what signal he should send:

"Tell 'em it's your birthday on Saturday," Ted shouted up. "I don't suppose they understand English any more than you know German; but it might give us a minute or two while they get their code books out."

"They vill not get the code books out," Captain Spengler said, and now there was a suggestion of fear in his voice." They vill varn guard ship lower down the fjord. That vill be finish of us."

"Guard ship!" Ted queried. "What sort of a tub is it?"

"Tub!" Spengler snapped. "It iss not a tub, but a small destroyer. She can blow us out of the water in seconds. I tell you, Sergeant, ve cannot get clear. It iss impossible."

"Don't know what the word impossible means," Ted replied woodenly. "Anyway, we're not being captured . . . so look to your steering, and don't forget I've got your little automatic here. Little but good, I'd say. It'll hurt if you force me to shoot."

A few moments later China was back at the wheel-house door.

"Curly sent me, Sarge. He says there's depth charges below, and he wants to know if you'd like some on deck. There are racks for rolling 'em over the stern."

"We're not likely to need depth charges," Ted began, then screwed up his eyes a little as a thought struck him. "Wait a minute. Yes, China, get some up. Put them on the racks. We may need 'em. Does it tell you how to set the fuses?"

China grinned.

"I'm not so good on German, Sarge. My weakness at college. I can say 'I love you' in French, Italian, Hindustani, Greek . . ."

"I'll take the rest as said," Ted snapped. "Set

the depth charges to go off, anyway. Curly should know something about them. He's done explosives."

China went, looking up at Sam who was forcing open an ammunition box so as to get his guns ready.

"How are you doing, Sam ? Happy ?"

"Will be when we get home. I'm thinking about that birthday cake. If I don't get home for Saturday . . . well, it won't do the thing any good to be left hanging around, will it ?"

"Oh, somebody'll eat it," China chuckled. "See you later."

The launch, one of Germany's latest, was thrumming along now leaving a great wash of disturbed water behind her. The white beam of the searchlight suddenly lit up towering cliffs ahead and Captain Spengler spun the wheel. The launch heeled smoothly and she changed course, and a few moments later they were running through the narrows. They had about six miles of fjord to traverse, and then they would be in salt water, with the North Atlantic ahead of them, and Scotland beyond the far horizon.

The high rocky walls flung back the thunder of the engines, and the sharp "Tac-a-tac-a-tac-tac-tac-tac" of the twin machine guns when Sam tried them out, warming them with short bursts. Each sixth bullet was a tracer, and these seemed to sail through the darkness quite slowly.

Suddenly Spengler lifted his hand to the searchlight and switched it off.

"What's the idea?" Ted asked, and added quickly: "Oh, I see."

They were emerging from the narrows, and ahead of them the darkness was sliced across by a brilliant searchlight beam. The guardship had apparently been warned by the signalling station, and nothing could pass down to the sea now without passing through that searchlight beam.

"All right, slow down," Ted ordered, and almost at once the bellowing thunder of the engines died down. The big launch still ploughed on, but at a command from Ted the bows were now turned towards the unseen destroyer.

"Take us alongside at quarter speed," Ted ordered, and to Sam on top he yelled: "Send China here, Sam, quick."

A few moments after Ted had given China his orders the launch was edging into the white beam, which moved a little until it was focused full on them.

With engines doing little more than turn-over the launch moved sedately towards the German ship. It was impossible to see the vessel, for the brilliant light made everything behind it completely black.

Ted called out to Sam:

"Don't let 'em see you, Sam, and when we go on our way . . . shoot out the searchlight. Okay ?"

"Okay, Sarge." Ted might have been ordering Sam to go across to the cook-house for a mug of tea for all the emotion there was in Sam's voice. He crouched down behind the machine-gun shield, and waited.

The light shining on them now illuminated everything so that the smallest print could have been read with ease.

Suddenly they were under the beam, and it was possible after a moment or so to see the vague outlines of the destroyer. Men lined her deck, and somebody hailed them in an angry, bellowing voice.

"Swing alongside . . . swing alongside," Ted ordered, and now the Italian automatic was pressing against Captain Spengler's spine. The German was no coward, but he knew that if he disobeyed this quiet-voiced Britisher he would die. These Commandos were playing a game of life and death. If they were taken prisoner they would probably die—Hitler had ordered it. If they escaped, what a triumph for them!

Spengler swung the launch expertly to port, and she was less than a fathom from the destroyer when Ted suddenly yelled:

"Now, China," and at the same moment he pulled both the switches he had watched Spengler move when he wanted full speed. The red lights winked quickly from red to green. The slight vibrations changed to a full-throated thrumming and at the same time there were four distinct splashes as four German depth charges rolled off the launch's ramps and into the water alongside the destroyer.

There were excited yells from the German ship. A challenge, then a whistle was blown shrilly. Men who had been standing watching the approach of the launch scampered madly to their guns, while the launch began to slide snakily into the night.

It was a matter of thirty seconds before a searchlight in the stern of the destroyer woke to life, and a beam began to probe the darkness, searching for the launch.

Ted had taken the precaution of making Spengler send their vessel first to the left and then to the right. He knew they could expect a devastating blast of small arms fire almost at once, and he was right. A heavy machine-gun began to yammer, vivid flashes of light winking in and out with bewildering rapidity. The launch swung out of the searchlight beam, but she could not answer the helm fast enough to dodge that broad white path of light.

Heavy machine-gun bullets began to smash into the launch. They smashed into the plating guarding Sam, and sent sparks of fire wheeling into the air. A twin light anti-aircraft unit was deflected in an effort to get shells down to them, but they screamed off into the night. Their turn would come when the launch got farther away.

In the wheel-house both Ted and Captain Spengler were lying down, and Ted had his fingers crossed and was praying that the depth charges would explode before a direct hit stopped the launch.

Sam fired a very short burst and then the guns jammed. With German bullets hammering at his gun-shield, and smashing into the planking about his feet he worked to free the jam.

Something like a hammer hit his foot, he cringed, but went on working. The gun was free. Crouched behind the shield which was now dented and buckled in a dozen places he peered through the range rings, then fired.

"Tat-tat-tat-tat-tat-tat-tat-tat-tat!" His guns added to the inferno of noise, and tracers from them seemed to fly slowly out into the darkness from which came that deadly brilliant white light.

Suddenly the light went out, and at the same moment Sam thought it had come on again, only this time with even added brilliance. A great white explosion seemed to light up his head, and then he was dropping into a dark, soft pit.

The moment the searchlight was put out of action Ted got to his knees and gave the wheel a half turn. The launch heeled smartly, and within seconds no more bullets were touching them. Sam had just about saved their bacon.

"Those rotten German depth-charges must have been duds," he snarled, and ordered Spengler to his feet. "Come on, pal, we're in a hurry. If that destroyer decides to follow us we're going to need all the start we can get."

"No start iss enough," Spengler gasped. "The destroyer can . . . *Gott!*"

The exclamation was jerked out of him as from the darkness astern there came a rumbling bellow, and as he looked back from the open wheel-house window he had a momentary vision of the destroyer lit up by a mighty explosion which was erupting from the dark waters. A second later there was another, then a third and a fourth. The depth charges had not been duds. The fuses had just been badly timed.

"I don't think that destroyer will follow us," Ted said, and wiped his hand across his chin. His face was dripping, and it was not spray. In those past hectic moments their lives had hung by a thread. That thread had looked like snapping, and would have been snapped if Sam Foster had not stayed up there, and shot out the searchlight.

For the next twenty minutes Ted stayed alongside Captain Spengler. Dawn was greying the snow-clad hills behind them. The steep hills on either side of the fjord were flattening out a little, and then they met the first of the salt waves.

In the grey of a winter's morning, with clouds so low that it would be next to impossible for aircraft to search for them, they rolled and bucketed out into the open sea.

Ted suddenly realised he was so thirsty he could have drunk a bucket of anything that was wet. He called up:

"Sam . . . Sam . . . come here a minute."

There was no reply. Ted hesitated for a moment then went to the wheel-house door, and looked up and back. The twin machine-guns were there. The shield was striped with silver where German bullets had knocked themselves out of shape against it.

Then a roll of the launch brought something else into sight. An arm which lolled helplessly, moving with each roll of the vessel, and Ted's heart gave a wild, sickening jump.

"Sam . . . for the love of mike open your eyes. Come on, lad, waken up, or it'll be too late."

As if from a great distance Sam heard the pleading voice of Curly Bates; but he did not "waken up"; he was comfortable; he was tired, and in any case what was Curly trying to waken him for? Curly went on for another minute, and then there was another voice. The second voice was clipped, hard, commanding.

"Private Foster, waken up, and be sharp about it, or you'll be late on parade."

Sam knew that voice, too. It belonged to Sergeant Ted Harris, and the sergeant sounded annoyed. Sam screwed up his eyes. He did not want to waken up. He felt tired, terribly tired, and his eyes were heavy as lead. Yet there would be trouble if he disobeyed Sergeant Harris. Besides he liked the *Sarge*. He would do anything for him.

With a great effort he managed to open his eyes a little, struggling hard to get back to full consciousness. He blinked as he saw Sergeant Ted Harris bending over him. Ted had sounded really annoyed, yet there was an anxious frown on his face; a frown which gave way to a smile when he saw that Sam's eyes were open.

"Here, drink this." Again it was a command, and Sam always obeyed commands from Sergeant Harris. He began to try to lift his right arm to take the cup; but before his arm could move somebody had lifted him into a partial sitting position, and the cup was at his lips. A moment later he was spluttering and coughing as something which tasted like molten metal was running down his throat. He shook his head when the cup was offered again.

"I said drink," Sergeant Harris snapped, and once more Sam obeyed orders.

This time he blinked. There was something about this drink which drove the heavy sleepiness away; it took the weariness out of his arms; drove the mists away from the brain.

The arm about his waist allowed him to relax again, and now Sergeant Harris was saying:

"You're feeling a lot better, Sam, and there's nothing to worry about. We're at sea, there's a mist on the water, so Jerry planes can't hunt us. In less than forty-eight hours we'll be home."

Sam opened his mouth in amazement.

"We got away?"

"Thanks to you. You put the Jerry gunners off by shooting out the searchlight just as they were really getting on the target. The depth charges stopped 'em from following us . . . but if the searchlight hadn't been shot out they'd have sunk us."

"What happened to me?" Sam asked. "I feel pretty dim."

"You stopped one, Sam," Ted explained gently. "We didn't have time to do anything for a few minutes and you lost a lot of blood. Anyway

. . . we've got you conscious again, and you'll stay conscious, Sam. You've got to swallow a lot of nourishment . . . and that's an order."

"Yes, Sarge." Sam did not feel like staying awake, but orders were orders, and those orders saved his life, for by keeping awake he could take the best nourishment the launch could provide.

On the Saturday morning, with a damp Scottish mist shrouding the coast, the German boat was guided through the protecting minefields by an Air-Sea-Rescue launch which had come out in response to a wireless signal. A doctor aboard gave Sam a blood transfusion.

One week later—six days after his birthday— Sam was sitting up and grinning at Sergeant Harris, Curly Bates, China Brown, and Nels Larssen. On a small table was the birthday cake, and a letter of congratulations from the G.O.C. Operation Lightning had been a success. Some of the men had not come back, but the rear-guard had done more than come back, they had brought with them a prize in the shape of one of the latest examples of Nazi coastal-defence launches.

"You've been Mentioned in Despatches, Sam," Sergeant Harris said, taking his second piece of cake and frowning at China Brown who was already wondering if he dare take a third piece. "And . . . er . . , you can have a job in the

cores if you like. I understand it'll be a few
weeks before you are fit for duty again. Then
there'll be seven days leave. Want a job in
Stores ?"

"Stores!" Sam looked from Sergeant Ted
Harris to China, then to Curly who was mopping
his bald head—it was rather warm in the hospital
ward. "Did you say Stores ?"

"Yes, a nice cushy job . . . handing out shirts,
vests, underpants . . . caps and so on."

"Are *you* going in Stores as well ?"

"What! Me ?" Sergeant Ted Harris almost
dropped his fruit cake in amazement. Then he
shook his head vigorously. "No . . . I dare say
there'll be other Commando jobs to do. I've
heard . . . but that's a secret, and you blokes
aren't to be trusted with secrets."

"Hm!" Sam leaned across the bed and lifted
what remained of the birthday cake off the plate
and nursed it between his knees. "Stores, eh!"
and there was indignation in his voice. "If
you shove me in Stores I'll . . . oh, get out of
here!"

"Here, Sam, Sam," Ted Harris chided, a chuckle
in his voice. "You can't talk like that to me.
Anyway, I didn't say you *had* to go into Stores.
You can go if you want."

"And if I don't want ?" Sam snapped.

"You come back to us," Ted informed him.

For a moment Sam pondered. Then he held up the cake again, a grin on his face.

"Have another piece," he suggested. "I'll be with you, as soon as they let me out of here. Stores . . . pah!"

THE END